Marlow:
Mango Run

Marlow:
Mango Run

Bill Craig

ABSOLUTELY AMAZING eBOOKS

Published by Whiz Bang LLC, 926 Truman Avenue, Key West, Florida 33040, USA.

Marlow: Mango Run copyright © 2014 by Gee Whiz Entertainment LLC. Electronic compilation/ print edition copyright © 2014 by Whiz Bang LLC.

For information contact:
Publisher@AbsolutelyAmazingEbooks.com

ISBN-13: 978-1497340824
ISBN-10: 1497340829

Absolutely Amazing eBooks
by Bill Craig

Rick Marlow Mysteries*

Marlow: Indigo Tide
Marlow: Banana Wind
Marlow: The Neon Goodbye
Marlow: Mango Run

Joe Collins Mysteries

The Butterfly Tattoo
Paradise Lost

* Available in popular ebook formats
as well as paperback.

To the Karaoke Gang at Montgomery's Steakhouse and to the fantastic wait staff there, from Michayla the Greeter to Tommy the Bartender and Mike Fairchild the KJ, and the servers Kristi, Laura, Michelle, Jackie et al.

Marlow:
Mango Run

Chapter One

Marlow ducked as the bullet hit the wooden wall and sent splinters flying in all directions. Behind him Andy whimpered and curled into a ball on the floor of the small fishing shack. Marlow waited until he could feel the tread of rubber-soled shoes on the wooden planking leading out from shore to where the shack stood on stilts that held it above the water.

The Escobars were coming. Marlow spun and leveled his revolver, the .38 bucking in his fist as he fired once, then a second time, before spinning back behind the wall. He heard a scream and then the sound of a body pitching into the water. There were curses in what he recognized as Spanish.

"Gringo! You are going to fucking die! Do you know this?" called a voice that he recognized as Simon. That meant he had shot Gomez.

"Fuck you, Simon. Too bad about Gomez," Marlow called back. Automatic weapons fire ripped through the wooden walls. Marlow dived on top of the young red-haired woman that had gotten him into this mess, protecting her body with his.

Marlow had three shots left in his revolver, but he had the comforting weight of the SCCY automatic that Walter Loomis had given him on a previous case in his pocket. It held 11 rounds in it. He hoped that it would be enough.

Simon was on the walkway. Marlow lifted the .38 and fired the last 3 rounds. He heard Simon mutter a guttural curse. Splinters exploded from the doorframe and filled the air. Marlow shoved the .38 into his waistband as he dragged the 9mm auto out of his left hand pants pocket. Marlow switched hands.

The double action only 9mm was clenched in his right fist, chamber-loaded and ready to fire. Simon was coming. He could feel it. Marlow shook his head remembering back where it all began...

Marlow was sitting at the Hogsbreath, looking out over the marina when his cell phone buzzed. Marlow pulled it out and looked at the number. It was Walter Loomis, the lawyer that had hired him and given him a chance by making him his investigator after he had come to Key West in disgrace from New York. "Yes Walter," Marlow answered the phone.

"Ricky, I have a client here for you. Could you come back to the office right away?" Walter asked.

"I'll be right there," Marlow broke the connection.

Recently Marlow had solved the case that had driven him from New York in shame and had avenged his father's death as well as his own shooting and the frame up that had followed. That victory and working with Dr. Jessica Harmon had helped him conquer some of the demons that fueled his addictions to tobacco and alcohol. He had cut down to five cigarettes a day and only occasionally anything stronger than beer to drink. He was running nearly half a mile now, a long way from where he had been before he had been shot originally. But it was progress.

Baby steps. His watchwords since coming to Key West. His face, arms, and legs were tanned. Today he was wearing a pale green guayubera shirt over a white ribbed tank top and a pair of olive drab cargo shorts. His .38 was clipped inside his waistband. His brown hair was now streaked with blond and he sported a two-day growth of stubble on his cheeks and chin. A pair of dark lensed sunglasses covered his blue eyes.

The sun was hot but the sea breeze made it seem less so as he stepped out into the street. His bicycle was chained out front and he bent down and unlocked the lock and freed the chain, then coiled it around the rod beneath the seat and refastened the lock to hold it there.

Even though it was several hours until sunset, Mallory Square was already crowded. Marlow wondered how many of them would hang around for the Sunset Celebration. He calculated that maybe half. The other half would have lost interest and moved on into the shops or bars.

The breeze ruffled his hair as he turned and peddled back towards the house that served as both residence and office for Walter Loomis, Attorney at Law. It also housed Marlow's own office, since he was Walter's chief investigator. For Walter to call him, he figured that it meant that they had a client.

He wondered what this case would bring. So far he had dealt with art thieves, blackmailers, foreign agents, white supremacists, and killers. He shook his head. In Key West one never knew.

The cooler air in the office was an immediate relief from the heat outside. Lola Ponsberry, Walter's long time secretary looked up from the reception desk. An older woman she was still vivaciously built and she loved her boss and Walter was finally starting to admit that he reciprocated her feelings. Lola's red hair was up in a very business-like bun.

"He's waiting Rick. A new client," Lola whispered.

"Any idea what it's about?" Marlow asked. He grabbed a mug and filled it with coffee, adding sweetener.

"A missing girl I think," Lola shrugged. Marlow winked at her and headed for the conference room door. He tapped on it with his knuckles and was called inside.

Walter Loomis was wearing a pale blue tropical weight suit over a white shirt and a pastel blue tie. His white hair was slicked back and parted on the right. He had a pair of reading glasses perched on the end of his nose as he looked at papers in a Manila folder. There was a color photograph paper clipped to what appeared to be a copy of a police report.

Marlow turned his attention to the couple sitting across from the white haired lawyer that was like a second father to him. The man was thin and balding, with a fringe of brown hair encircling his head. He wore a worn black suit and a white shirt. His black tie was loosened and tugged down to half-mast no doubt due to the heat. The woman with him that Marlow assumed was his wife was wearing a floral print dress that reached to her knees sitting and that he was sure would hang beneath them if she had been standing. She wore short white gloves and white flats that would do nothing to accentuate her legs. Her hair had been red once but was faded to a whitish gray.

4

"Ricky my boy, please come in," Walter pushed to his feel. "Mister and Mrs. Gables. Harold and Natasha, this is Rick Marlow my investigator."

"A pleasure to meet you both," Marlow told them. He took a sip of his coffee as he sat down at the large table. "How can I help?"

"Ricky, the Gables daughter, Andrea is missing. They believe that she has runaway," Walter explained.

"How old is she?" Marlow asked.

"She's sixteen," Mrs. Gables said softly.

"A rough age," Marlow nodded.

"A disrespectful age you mean. That girl refused to listen anyone," Harold sniffed disdainfully. Marlow decided right then that he didn't like the man.

"Andy is strong-willed," Natasha Gables shot her husband a dirty look.

"How so?" Marlow asked.

"She has a mind of her own and thinks for herself. He doesn't like that so much," Natasha Gables nodded towards her husband.

"Why is that, Mr. Gables?" Marlow asked, his eyes searching the man's face.

"Girls that age need to mind their manners, be seen and not heard. I don't hold with all these new fangled ideas of letting kids do what they want and express themselves. It just leads to anarchy and chaos," Harold Gables shook his head.

"You dislike new ideas?" Marlow took another sip of his coffee.

"I dislike a lot of things," Harold said sourly.

"I can see that," Marlow nodded.

"What is that supposed to mean?"

"Just that I can see you dislike a lot of things."

"Don't go getting snotty with me, boy," Harold's tone held a warning of violence.

"I wouldn't dream of it," Marlow held out both hands in a conciliatory gesture.

"Can you find our little girl?" Natasha asked.

"I can try," Marlow told her. He liked Natasha Gables. He could tell that her concern for her daughter was genuine. He had a feeling that her husband considered the daughter's absence as a blessing.

"I can have a contract drawn up within the hour," Walter interjected.

"How much is this going to cost me?" Harold Gables demanded.

"A five hundred dollar retainer and $100.00 dollars a day plus expenses," Marlow replied.

"He said you charged by the hour," Harold nodded towards Walter.

"I like your wife, so you get a discount," Marlow said.

"What does that mean," Harold's eyes narrowed in anger.

"It means I am doing it for her, not you," Marlow met his gaze.

"Harold!" Natasha put her hand on her husband's arm. He looked ready to explode and then slumped in the chair in defeat.

"Let me write a check," Harold Gables sighed. He pulled out a worn brown leather checkbook and opened it. He acted as if he was in physical pain as he wrote out the check for the retainer. He tore it out and entered it in his ledger and then sailed it across the desk at Walter. "We are at The Pier House. Send the contract over and I'll sign it." Gables said.

Marlow said nothing as Harold stood and stalked out of the room. He turned his eyes towards Natasha Gables. "Don't judge him too harshly. Harold is a proud man and Andy hasn't made it easy on him," she said.

"Why is that?" Marlow asked.

"Natasha! Come on!" Harold yelled from the door.

"I have to go now, Mr. Marlow. We'll talk more later," Natasha told him as she stood. Picking up her purse she strode purposely from the room.

"Wow. What do you make of all that?" Marlow looked at Walter.

"I'll let you know after I see if the check clears. Would you like to deliver the contract?" Walter replied.

"I would. Something smells, Walter."

"I agree," Walter nodded. "Do you want to see her picture and read the initial police report?"

"I probably should," Marlow slid the folder across the table and opened it. He pulled out the picture of Andrea Gables. She was a pretty girl with a pale complexion and long red hair. Green eyes. She reminded Marlow of the girl that played the writer's daughter on the television show Castle.

Walter left the conference room to have Lola pull out a standard contract and get the proper names and dollar amounts typed into it. He had tried to get his boss to computerize more but Walter stubbornly remained wedded to typewritten documents. Marlow dug his pack of cigarettes out of his pocket and shook one free. He looked at it a minute, trying to remember how many this would make. One after breakfast, one after lunch. This would be three. Marlow dug out his lighter and fired it up, drawing the smoke into his lungs and then blowing it out. He put the lighter back in his pocket.

Marlow picked up the police report. It contained the dry facts of the case. Harold Gables was on Key West working on the refurbishment of one of the historical buildings. Originally the Gable family was from Big Pine Key. According to the report, Andrea had started hanging out with a local guy named Phil, no last name. He was older and paid her a lot of attention. It was a story Marlow had heard a hundred times before as a cop up in the Big Apple. She had been gone for three days now and the Key West cops didn't seem to be giving it much attention.

Runaways were all over the island. If they didn't want to be found, it was difficult. Phil was described as a surfer type with blond hair and blue eyes, shaggy haired and tats covering both of his arms. Sounded like half the guys on the goddamn beaches. Except there were only wind-surfers on Key West. It was a possibility.

The only saving grace was the fact that Andrea was under age. That was leverage on a guy like Phil. If he could find him. Faced with statutory rape and carrying a sex-offender rap for the rest of his life would be a strong incentive to tell what he knew.

Marlow noticed that Phil was said to hang out on Stock Island. Not the best of places to be, but if the guy felt at home there it would be worth checking out. He thought about calling his girlfriend, Della Martin. She was a detective on the Key West police department. Still missing persons was not her normal detail. The thought of involving Chief Learner was enough to make Marlow want to throw up. Especially since the Chief seemed to have already written this one off. Marlow wasn't so sure though.

He had a gut feeling about Natasha Gables. She could tell him a lot more about her daughter than any photograph. He had a feeling she could tell him a lot more about her daughter than the police report could. And she could tell him about the tension between her and her husband and between her daughter and the husband.

Marlow looked at the picture again. Was Harold molesting Andrea? Was that why she had run? He stubbed out his cigarette in the crystal ashtray.

"Well?" Walter asked as he waddled back into the room.

"I think I need to find the boyfriend first. He will lead us to the girl," Marlow told him.

"I agree, Ricky. Lola should have the contract ready in about fifteen minutes," Walter told him.

"Good, because I have plenty of questions about this one," Marlow said.

Chapter Two

The sun was beating down on him as Marlow peddled over to the Pier House. He was hoping to get a chance to speak with Natasha Gables alone about her daughter but he wasn't counting on it. He had called Della but she had not been able to give him anything beyond what had been in the initial missing person's report.

Sweat ran down his face as he peddled, but it was from honest labor and not just from the heat. Della had been able to add little to his knowledge of Phil, but had instead passed him over to Danny Otero, a vice detective that had been able to tell him more. Otero had informed Marlow that his last name was Gordon and that he lived on Stock Island. That fact alone made Marlow feel a little hesitant. Stock Island was becoming a bad place to hang out unless one was involved with drugs.

If Phil Gordon was well known on Stock Island, it meant that he was connected with heavy hitters. That would be for Marlow to determine during the course of his investigation. If Andrea Gables had hooked up with Phil, she likely was on Stock Island, which was where Marlow would head after he talked to her mother.

The Pier House seemed slightly more formidable than when Larry Smith played in the Piano Bar. The new owners had closed the room though Larry had negotiated to purchase the piano he had spent so much time with.

Marlow was one of many who were less than happy with the change. It was almost like when the Key West *Citizen* had discontinued the *Solares Hill*, which had turned his friend Thom Hark back into a feature reporter.

Marlow had no doubt his old friend would manage to bounce back from the temporary setback. Still, as a feature reporter, Thom might well be able to provide even more information than he had before. The British ex-pat had an almost encyclopedic memory about Key West and its government.

Marlow locked his bike and entered the Pier House. The expansive lobby looked very corporate and sterile. It was a look Marlow had never liked. He missed Larry's playing, though he could be caught at one of many other musical venues on the island. Marlow stopped at the desk and had them ring the Gables and let them know he was on his way up.

Harold Gables opened the door with the same pinched and sour expression that he had worn at the office. Except now he was dressed in work clothes and looked more comfortable. "Where's the contract?" he grumbled. Marlow handed it to him and he signed where it was indicated and handed it back to Marlow. "I need to get back to work," he said and headed out the door.

"Please excuse Harold's rudeness. Work it seems is all he cares about these days," Natasha Gables said. She hadn't changed clothes and was holding a bottle of water.

"I had the impression that there were things you wanted to tell me about your daughter," Marlow said.

"Andy is a good girl, but we had her later than most. Harold is very old-fashioned in many respects and he doesn't understand what it is like for a young teenaged girl to live in such a restrictive atmosphere. So she has been rebellious. It has gotten worse since she sees the way people are here on Key West. Big Pine is more conservative. Then she met Phil," Natasha shook her head and took another sip of water.

"Do you know where and how they met?" Marlow asked.

"She was on one of the beaches, she told me. And he was windsurfing. He was attractive and he didn't seem to mind her age. It was innocent enough at first, buying her a soft drink and just sitting and talking. Then he started teaching her to surf. After that she began slipping out at all hours to meet him. She told me she knew what she was doing and that she could handle him. Then three days ago she didn't come home and I haven't heard from her since.

"Harold didn't even want to go to the police. Good riddance he said. I hated him at that moment. I wanted to stick a knife in him. She's my little girl! I made Harold go to the police and then I made him go to your boss. He hated it. Once I have Andy back, I plan on leaving him," Natasha confessed.

"I will do my best to find her," Marlow told her.

"I know you will. Thank you, Mr. Marlow," Natasha Gables looked at him, tears streaming down her cheeks.

"Call me Rick, or Marlow. Mr. Marlow was my father," Marlow told her. She slumped against him and he wrapped his arms around her and let her cry. There was really nothing more that he could do.

Harold Gables walked through the job site. So far everything was on schedule despite the aggravation that his wife was putting him through. He hoped that his bosses on the job would understand. Simon and Gomez Escobar had reputations for being very hard if a job wasn't done to perfection and on time.

He was actually surprised to see that Gomez was on site. Gomez Escobar was a handsome man with curly dark hair, brown eyes and light brown skin. Gomez had a goatee with very little white showing. He was dressed in a suit that Harold knew he would never be able to afford in a hundred years and was surrounded by three large bodyguards.

"Mr. Escobar, how nice to see you," Harold called out as he approached. Gomez Escobar turned to face him, smiling and showing perfect white teeth.

"Harold, my friend! It looks like things are coming along nicely," Gomez told him after surveying the work that had been done on the property.

"The club should be ready to open as scheduled," Harold acknowledged.

"Good! How about your personal problem, Harold?" Gomez asked.

"Fucking kid ran off and the wife is shitting her pants about it. She made me hire a private detective to hunt for her. It's a fucking waste of money," Harold shook his head.

"Will this bring bad publicity for the opening of our club?" Gomez asked.

"It shouldn't," Harold shook his head.

"I hope not, Harold. Bad publicity will preclude us from hiring you again for future projects," Gomez said flatly.

"There won't be any problems, Mr. Escobar," Harold assured him.

"I hope not, Harold. I hope not," Escobar said.

Marlow was sitting on the beach, drinking a bottle of water and watching the wind-surfers. So far he had not seen Phil Gordon but he would keep looking. He had a good description of the guy, but so far he had not found him on the beaches where he had been looking. The sun was setting and he was tired of wasting time.

Andrea Gables had been missing for three days. Marlow was afraid of what he might find. Too many times runaways gone that long ended up dead, found in an alley with their throat slit and raped brutally. He didn't want Andy Gables to end up that way.

The sun was sinking into the gulf and Marlow decided to check out the hot spots. There was a good chance that he might run into Phil somewhere on Key West.

There were things that he didn't like about Harold Gables. Things he wasn't sure he believed about what Natasha Gables had told him. Something was being held back from him. Important information. Marlow wondered what it was.

Marlow dusted the sand off his butt as he stood up and walked away. He dropped the empty plastic water bottle in a public trashcan on the beach. Marlow headed for Mallory Square and the daily sunset celebration where people looked south hoping to catch a glimpse of the fabled green flash.

The Green Flash was supposed to foretell good luck and good fortune for any who saw it. It was a local superstition but one that many believed. Marlow headed down Duvall Street and saw Toltec, the loincloth clad Mayan with the parrot on each shoulder dancing for the tourists on the corner in front of Sloppy Joe's. Inside a local country and western band had their speakers turned up loud enough that they could be heard on the street.

Marlow headed inside. He was aggravated at his not being able to find Phil during the day and he wondered why that was? Even though he had asked about Phil Gordon, nobody had been willing to talk. That in and of itself was unusual. The fact that nobody was willing to talk about Phil was a clue in and of itself.

More and more it was looking like he would have to make a trip to Stock Island. Marlow wasn't ready for that yet. It wasn't that he was afraid, far from it. Stock Island reminded Marlow of the wild wild west back in the days before Dodge City was tamed.

Stock Island had a reputation for being a bad place to hang out. Marlow sighed. It looked like he had little to no choice but to go there in his search for Andrea Gables.

The sun was setting as he peddled back to Walter's with the signed contract. Walter had texted to let him know that the check had cleared. Marlow was glad to hear it. It meant beer money if he and Della went out. It also meant that if he had to spread some cash around on Stock Island, he could.

Marlow had a feeling that Phil Gordon might not want to be found. Asking directly could bring more trouble than it was worth from well meaning friends. No, he would have to be careful in his search for the surfer. Marlow sighed. He hated working undercover, but he really couldn't see any other way to approach it. He would talk to Walter and see what he thought.

Della Martin rubbed her temples. It had been a long day. She was looking forward to sharing a couple of cold beers with Marlow at the Schooner later. Winter brought an earlier sunset and the onset of hurricane season.

Della was impressed with the progress that Marlow had made with Dr. Harmon. Of course, finding the person that had ordered him shot and his father killed might have had just as much to do with it.[1] It was an enormous event, and in an of itself could have had a lot to do with relieving the Post Traumatic Stress Syndrome that Marlow had refused to deal with for years.

She was even more impressed with the discipline Marlow was showing in cutting down on his addiction to tobacco. He had gone from half a pack a day to 5 cigarettes a day. That was major progress from the 3 packs a day he had been smoking when he first came to Key West.

Marlow had even managed to quit drinking Vodka straight, at least most of the time. The few nights she had spent at his apartment, she knew he still had nightmares. But they were not as bad as before.

---

[1] The Neon Goodbye

Della picked up her cell phone and dialed Marlow's number. She wondered if he wanted her to pick him up...

Stock Island, Florida

Phil Gordon twisted the top off the bottle of Budweiser and took a long pull. He thought about Andy Gables. Ready and willing, in a big hurry to grow up. He climbed out of the pick-up truck in front of the ramshackle cabin where he lived and she waited. It hadn't taken him long to get her hooked on Heroine and then Cocaine. His boss was pleased with the rapid way he had brought her along.

He had been surprised at the personal interest that the boss had shown in this girl. He wondered about that. God knew she was pretty as hell. Pretty decent in the sack after he had taught her a few things. He drained half the Bud as he walked to the door. "Hey Andy, Daddy's home!" Phil called.

The television was on inside the cabin. Phil slammed the screen door open as he walked inside. He heard movement and saw her struggling to stand. She was wearing a white cotton slip he had given her. From the lamp behind her she wore nothing else. He could see the outline of her pert little breasts and the curve of her hips through the cotton gown.

He couldn't even remember what he had done with the clothes she had been wearing when he brought her to the cabin on Stock Island. "Hey Angel, did you miss me? Daddy brought some presents," He waved two glassine envelopes in front of her. Andy licked her lips in anticipation. "You come over here and make me happy and then I'll make you happy," Phil told her.

Andy dropped to her knees and reached out and unzipped his pants. He groaned with pleasure as he felt her hands on him. He could feel his skin stretching as he became hard. Her hands encircled him and then he felt her tongue licking him and then her mouth surrounded him and it began to move up and down...

Key West, Florida

"I don't like it Ricky. Stock Island is bad news," Walter Loomis said, leaning back in his chair, his hands entwined over his prestigious belly.

"It is, but if that is where the girl is likely to be found," Marlow shrugged.

"It is a theory," Walter said.

"Only until I check it out."

\"Why are you doing this, Ricky?"

"I like Mrs. Gables. She cares about her daughter," Marlow shrugged, lighting his fourth cigarette of the day.

"What do you think of the father?" Walter asked.

"He's a jerk," Marlow shrugged, blowing smoke.

"That he is," Walter sighed.

Chapter Three

The night was bright and loud as Marlow and Della entered The Schooner. Marlow noticed a local celebrity, a journalist named Murphy at the bar and nodded. Thom Hark had introduced them one day at The Chart Room. He nodded at Murphy and got a nod back in return as the man puffed on a fat cigar.

"Rough day, Marlow?" Della asked as they took a seat and a waitress came to take their order. After the waitress left Marlow took out his fifth cigarette of the day and showed it to her.

"Last one of the day. And yes, it has been a bit rough. Anytime you deal with assholes is," Marlow shrugged as he pulled out his lighter and fired up the cigarette.

"How are the sessions with Dr. Harmon going?" Della asked lightly. She knew how hard Marlow had fought against going to see the psychiatrist.

"Better than I expected," Marlow exhaled smoke.

"I know I'm not supposed to ask, Rick, but with everything that happened..." Della didn't finish.

"I can't discuss it with you Della. Just like you can't discuss your sessions either. Not only would Dr. Harmon not approve, it could set us both back in the course of our treatment," Marlow tapped off some ash. Della was also seeing Dr. Harmon for PTSD after being shot on a case involving Marlow.[2]

[2] Marlow: Banana Wind

"I know, Rick. But...it's hard not knowing. Maybe it's being a cop, I don't know," Della shook her head.

"I have the same curiosity. I just don't voice it," Marlow shrugged.

"How do you do that?"

"It is just something that I do. I don't think about it. Maybe it's a guy thing. Compartmentalization, something like that," Marlow puffed on his cigarette. The waitress arrived with their drinks and Marlow paid for them and included a five-dollar tip.

"How about this new case and the guy you were asking me about?" Della took a pull on her beer.

"Phil Gordon. I think he might be a predator who has something to do with the disappearance of a teenage girl. I know he is based on Stock Island thanks to what your friend in Vice told me," Marlow explained.

"So what are you going to do?"

"I am going to spend some time on the beaches soaking up sun. The guy is a wind-surfer. He'll turn up," Marlow shrugged as he took a drink and tapped off more ash.

"That's your plan? Marlow, the only surfers on Key West are wind surfers. Shorter boards attached to big kites," Della looked at him.

"Best one I have for the moment, but that is good to know."

"Wow."

"My sentiments exactly." Marlow took a pull on his Killian's Red.

Marlow had dropped Della off at her place and was sitting in front of the television. He had caught a re-run of The Rockford Files from a satellite station in Miami. He poured himself half of a six-ounce tumbler of Vodka. He had added a couple of ice cubes to it as well.

Rockford had just walked out of his trailer with a buddy and somebody started shooting. Marlow took a drink and then toasted the television. He agreed with Jim Rockford that getting shot was not a fun thing.

The missing person case was bothering him. There was more going on in the Gables household than what he was being told. He didn't buy the father's attitude of good riddance to bad rubbish. No, he wasn't getting a good vibe from the father at all. He was pretty sure that the father had more to do with the girl being a runaway than even the mother knew.

Sadly it was an old story, one he had seen many times as a beat cop back in New York City. The father is tired of the wife, the daughter is developing and catches his eye. Young, pert, untouched. Marlow shook his head and took a drink. The beers earlier had tasted good, but this was better.

Still, he would limit himself to two. He was working. Limits. Baby steps. Just enough to take the edge off, enough to help him sleep. Despite his work with Dr. Harmon, despite finally closing the case on his shooting, Marlow still had nightmares.

He still went back to that alley, the snow falling down. Standing over a brother officer. Hearing his partner tell him he was sorry. Hearing the shots as he turned and feeling the hammer-blows to his chest as the bullets

23

struck. Seeing Nolan holding the gun in his hands as he fell backwards into the snow. Hearing Nolan call "Officer Down," into his radio and then that final shot. The snowflakes falling down on his face and into his eyes.

Marlow blinked three times and took a drink. He swished it around in his mouth before swallowing it. He could feel the warmth spreading in his belly. He drained the glass and poured himself another. Marlow shut off the television and put a new disc in the CD player. Art Pepper's Winter Moon. Marlow liked the title cut, but his favorite was When the Sun Comes Out. It had been covered many times by the likes of Judy Garland and Ella Fitzgerald, but Marlow preferred the instrumental version.

He thought about a cigarette, but he had finished his fifth one at the bar with Della. Smoking another was out of the question. Marlow took another drink, his eyelids finally feeling heavy. Marlow finished the drink, put his tumbler in the sink and went to bed. Art Pepper was the last thing he heard before drifting off to sleep...

Marlow was up before the sun despite his late night. He pulled on shorts and a tank top. He slipped a .22 automatic into the pocket of his shorts. Marlow had been in the business long enough not to take chances. Too many enemies. Marlow tied his running shoes and headed out the door. He jogged to the beach. It wasn't far to the beach.

Marlow jogged along the beach. This was probably his favorite time of day. Jogging along the beach, the waves washing up on the sand. A soft breeze blowing in off the sea.

Marlow fought for breath. He was pushing himself, pushing harder than he had before. Half a mile. Still running. Pushing. Marlow fell to the ground gasping for breath. His lungs were burning as he heaved the meager contents of his stomach into the sand. Fortunately he had not eaten yet.

Still, it was better than the day before. Once he had caught his breath, Marlow climbed to his feet. He thought about the Gable case and he was sure that he was right. Marlow walked home and showered and dressed again and headed for Harpoon Harry's for breakfast. After that, on to the beach.

At least today he had a specific destination. Smathers Beach. It was the one that most of the wind-surfers frequented. Smathers Beach is one of four beaches within the City. As one of the largest beaches, best known for its spring breaks. It houses restrooms and shower facilities along with volleyball courts, a boat ramp and Jet Ski rentals. It seemed like the kind of place Phil would frequent.

Marlow peddled out. Cars would be out of place. He would fit in far better as just another castaway at the End of the Road. The End of the Road. He had heard Key West called that many times since his arrival. Literally it was the truth since the island was the southernmost part of the United States. Aside from the Conchs that were life-long residents, it had the largest transient population of the United States. People drifted in and out. Some stayed for awhile, then they moved on. Others came and stayed, though they never put down permanent roots, living under bridges and in hedges or boxes in alleyways.

Marlow figured he was fortunate to have a roof over his head and a bed to sleep in. If not for Walter, he wouldn't have. He had been near the end of his funds and the end of his rope when Walter Loomis had offered him the job as his chief investigator. Marlow had taken the job and never looked back.

Except when he had to. Like the last case. He had been forced to solve his own shooting. He had managed it, but not without a price. Coming face to face with one's killer was hard at best, and when that same person had killed his father as well, it made it worse. Still it had cleared the books on three shootings in New York and several in Key West as well.

Marlow rolled his bike into the rack and secured the chain and padlock. He wore a fanny pack which concealed his .38 as well as cash for food and drinks. Marlow had added a white Corona cap with palm trees to his apparel. His bottled water was wet with condensation as he unscrewed the top and took a long pull from the bottle.

He had seen the Wind-surfers out on the few waves rolling in on the few waves. Marlow planned to meet them and find out much more about them. The wind was blowing at about fifteen miles an hour. Marlow wasn't nautical enough to convert that into knots per hour but he figured it meant that the kite-boarders would be able to get a decent ride. He had Googled the term windsurfer on-line and had the Wikipedia definition: Windsurfing is a surface water sport that combines elements of surfing and sailing. It consists of a board usually 2 to 3 meters long, with a volume of about 60 to 250 liters, powered by wind on a sail. The rig is connected to the board by a free-rotating universal joint and consists of a mast, 2-sided boom and sail. The sail area generally ranges from 2.5 m² to 12 m² depending on the conditions, the skill of the sailor and the type of windsurfing being undertaken.

Some credit S. Newman Darby with the origination of windsurfing by 1965 on the Susquehanna River, Pennsylvania, USA when he invented the "sailboard", which, incidentally, he did not patent

Marlow carried a bottle of water with him. A white Corona baseball cap covered his sun-streaked hair. His .38 rested in a Special Weapons Products fanny pack around his waist. His orange Aloha shirt hung loosely on his shoulders over the white wife-beater ribbed tank top that was tucked into his cargo shorts.

The wind-surfers kept well away from the rest of Smathers Beach, where the beach volleyball courts and swimmers held court. Marlow dropped to the sand sitting and watching as the boarders unloaded their gear and assembled the kites and masts and booms. Most of them paddled out with the sails and booms laid flat on the boards. Once they were out from shores they would raise the sails and ride the combination of wind and wave that gave them their thrills.

It was ten o'clock in the morning. The sun was shinning the temperature was about 86 degrees. Most of the wind-surfers were skipping across the waves. Marlow continued to watch, looking for anybody that matched Phil's description. He was about ready to call it a day when a black Dodge Ram pulled into the parking area and a guy pulled out and started hauling gear out of the back.

Marlow stood and walked towards the guy. He unscrewed the bottle cap and took a long pull before re-capping the bottle and sticking it into his cargo pocket.

"Need a hand?" Marlow called.

"I could use one," the guy admitted.

"You got a cool rig. I'm wanting to learn," Marlow told him ad he pulled the mast with the sail and lines wrapped around it out of the bed of the truck. The guy hauled out his own board and Marlow took note of the tattoos on the guy's arms.

"It's a rush for sure. Better than surfing if you ask me. Surfing you deal with the waves, wind surfing, you gotta fight the wind and the waves," the guy shrugged.

"I'm Marlow," he said, introducing himself.

"Phil. You got an outfit Marlow?" Phil asked.

"Not yet. Figured it would be good to line up a teacher first," Marlow shrugged,

"Not a bad idea," Phil agreed.

"That's what I thought," Marlow nodded.

"You really want to learn?" Phil asked as they reached the water.

"I do," Marlow told him, realizing he meant it.

"Watch me today, then tomorrow I'll take you around to get you the best equipment," Phil told him, shaking Marlow's hand. He quickly talked Marlow through assembling the mast and sail to the board and how to work the lines, then Phil was in the water peddling out.

Marlow smiled as he watched him go. He had established contact.

Chapter Four

Marlow fired up a cigarette as he watched Phil windsurfing. From what he could tell, the guy was pretty good at it. He had an athlete's body, though the gut was starting to build. Marlow wondered what Phil did for a living. It was something he would be checking on if the guy didn't volunteer it.

His water bottle was almost empty so Marlow climbed to his feet as he smoked down the cigarette. The wind was starting to kick up some of the fine sand as he trudged up to one of the food trucks and bought a cold bottle of water. Marlow put out his cigarette in a public receptacle and unscrewed the top of the water bottle. He looked back out over the water as he took a long pull.

As hot as it was on the beach, the water tasted almost better than booze. Almost. He caught sight of Phil as the guy was making his board literally dance across the waves, weaving in and out of the other kite-boarders out there. Marlow trudged back to his spot in the sand and dropped back down to watch the intricate ballet that was the wind-surfers darting across and over the waves.

"He's bad news, you know," a soft voice said from beside him.

"Who is?" Marlow asked, turning his head to check out the young woman that had spoken to him first.

She was small, petite and blonde with light brown eyes that were peering at him over the top of a pair of Foster

Grant sunglasses. "Phil. Everybody down here knows it. You might have noticed, nobody came to help him get his gear to the water."

"I did notice. You got a name?"

"Sally. What about you?"

"Marlow. So what makes Phil bad news, Sally?"

"For one thing he's a bully. Likes to beat people up, doesn't matter if it's a guy or a girl. Most girls, unless they're really desperate, don't go out on a second date with him," Sally shrugged.

"He rough 'em up?" Marlow's voice had developed an edge and his eyes turned cold as he looked back out over the water.

"I know for a fact he doesn't take no for an answer. Except nobody ever presses charges. He makes it real clear what happens if they do," Sally said.

"Interesting."

"Some girls went out with him, they ain't been seen again. So most of us steer real clear of him. The others said I should mind my own business, but I liked your looks and I thought you ought' a know," Sally smiled at him. Marlow liked her smile.

"I'm glad you told me, Sally. Forewarned is forearmed. I know not to trust him now, so I'll be ready when he makes his move," Marlow told the girl.

"Just be careful," Sally told him solemnly as she stood and walked back to the group. Marlow took another pull at his water as his eyes coldly followed Phil across the water.

Marlow was on his third bottled water by the time Phil guided his board back to shore. Marlow stood and walked out to help him tear it down and carry it back to his truck.

Sally and her friends were long gone and Marlow was glad of it. He didn't want to see any of those kids caught in a crossfire if things went to hell.

"You were pretty good out there," Marlow observed as they carried stuff back to the truck.

"I got a sponsor to go compete out in California next month," Phil grinned, pushing his unruly mop of hair back out of his eyes.

"They have competitions?" Marlow asked.

"Hell yeah, this is actually recognized as a professional sport as well as an Olympic sport," Phil shrugged.

"I didn't know that. I just thought it looked like a lot of fun."

"It is that too."

"Hey, you want to grab a beer tonight? Maybe the Hogsbreath or The Schooner?" Marlow asked.

"Sure, what the hell. Meet me at the Green Parrot about eight. I hear they got a pretty rocking band playing tonight," Phil grinned, shaking Marlow's hand.

"Eight o'clock," Marlow nodded. He made sure to memorize the license plate of Phil's truck as he drove off. Marlow headed for his bike and peddled back to the office.

"So what did you learn, Ricky?" Walter Loomis asked.

"Actually more than I hoped for," Marlow replied as he poured himself a cup of coffee. He poured in two packets of sweetener and stirred it in. Marlow took a sip.

"Explain," Walter looked at him.

"Phil Gordon is very well known on Smathers' Beach. Even the young girls know to avoid him because of his reputation. That would be a big draw for someone like Andy Gables," Marlow shrugged.

"Why?" Walter looked at him.

"He's a bad boy. Girls that go out with him sometimes don't come back. Most know him as a rapist. But anyone that tries to have him prosecuted, they suddenly disappear," Marlow explained.

"This scares me, Ricky," Walter told him.

"It does me too, Walter. But that girl is in trouble. I won't be able to live with myself if I don't try to help her," Marlow said.

"While I understand, it doesn't make me feel any better," Walter sighed.

"I know that. I'm meeting him for beers at The Green Parrot later," Marlow said.

"Do you really think that is wise?" Walter asked.

"I don't see that I have a choice if I want to find Andy Gables," Marlow told him.

"Good point," Walter nodded.

Andy Gables was hurting. It had been a long time since her last fix. She withered on the floor like a snake with its head cut off. Hopefully Phil would be back soon with what she needed. The pain was terrible. Andy clawed at her arms, drawing blood.

It forced moments of clarity on her, Harold on top of her, forcing himself inside her as she fought against him. Her mother knew, but she did nothing! Andy screamed as she felt her stepfather piercing her, filling her with his flesh and seed...

Marlow had his .38 clipped inside the holster in his waistband, covered by his shirt as he made his way along Duval Street. There were a lot of places that he could have stopped before, but he didn't. Marlow headed straight to the Green Parrot. He went inside and ordered a beer.

Phil Gordon watched dispassionately as the men loaded Andy onto the truck. They would take her to Miami where she would learn what it took to become a mule for the Escobar brothers. She was a good fuck, and he would miss her. But he wouldn't miss her all that much.

The band was a country band and Marlow enjoyed the music. He hated to think that it was for nothing. Marlow loved country music, but it still wasn't his favorite. Jazz was his favorite. The country band did its bit and that was fine.

Marlow was on his third beer when Phil finally showed up. Marlow was on his fourth cigarette of the day, and had nearly finished it as he spotted the wind-surfer. Marlow ground the butt out in the ashtray on the bar. Marlow looked at his watch.

"Yeah I know I'm late. I had to load some stuff on a truck to Miami. Took longer than I thought it would," Phil shrugged, waving down the bartender.

"Hate when that happens," Marlow took a pull on his beer. He had been waiting nearly two hours and it had been a long day.

"So about tomorrow? You going to be on-time then?" Marlow asked.

"Yeah Dude, why you so bent out of shape. I told you I got tied up," Phil's voice took on an edge.

"I just don't like wasting my time. I'm willing to pay for the lessons. If not from you, then somebody else," Marlow replied coldly.

"I thought you were a cool guy, Marlow. I guess I was wrong," Phil's face was getting red.

"I thought you were too until I asked around about you Phil. The girls on the beach, they do like to talk. Especially about friends who go out on dates with you and don't come back," Marlow said calmly.

"Bunch a lying bitches! Well fuck you, Pal!" Phil yelled.

"You ain't my type. No real man would hit a woman or threaten one," Marlow turned partially away from Phil but he knew what was coming. His hand wrapped around the long neck bottle of his Killian's Red. Phil threw a punch but Marlow dodged it and brought the half full bottle around and grinned as it exploded across Phil's face. Phil screamed as the shattering glass cut his cheek.

Phil came up with a blade in his hand and slashed at Marlow. Marlow ducked inside the knife and rammed the broken bottle into Phil's knife arm. The blade clattered to the floor as Phil bent over. Marlow kicked him in the face and Phil hit the floor. Marlow threw two twenty's on the bar and walked out. He wanted Phil out of commission for a few hours. Both the guy's face and arm would require stitches. While he was getting them, Marlow planned on checking his place out.

He had reached Stock Island by the time the ambulance arrived at The Green Parrot to pick Phildo the dildo up. Marlow had managed to get Phil's address from Della's friend in Vice. Marlow coasted down the mud and gravel road to the isolated fishing shack where Phil lived.

There were no lights on in the wooden shack. It in and of itself was something of a rarity. Aside from the hospital, most of the homes on Stock Island were aluminum trailers. The blue-collar population of Key West lived over here. Carpenters, boat builders, fishermen. Most were good people, just poor. Poor in a money sense, but rich in family and the things that really mattered.

Marlow climbed off his bike and put down the kickstand. He drew his .38 as he made his way up onto the wooden front porch. Marlow moved as quietly as he could but the ancient wooden boards creaked under his weight. He tried the doorknob. It turned easily under his hand. Marlow shoved the door open and waited.

It was pitch black inside the shack. Marlow was prepared for that. He removed a flat black object from his pocket and then clicked a release button. An object popped out. Marlow squeezed it and light flashed from a led bulb. Marlow cranked the lever and the white beam became brighter. The white beam sliced through the darkness. Marlow searched the house. Andy was gone, but Marlow found evidence that she had been there. The clothes that she had been wearing when she disappeared.

Marlow took pictures with his Nokia phone and then stepped outside and called the Key West Police Department.

Chief Tom Learner was the first to arrive, Della Martin was right behind him. "What the fuck is going on Marlow?" Learner demanded.

"I have evidence that a guy that lives here, a guy by the name of Phil Gordon, kidnapped and held against her will a girl I was hired to find," Marlow replied. He was on his last cigarette of the day.

"Would that be the same Phil Gordon that you assaulted in The Green Parrot earlier tonight?" Learner asked.

"I have no idea what you're talking about Tom," Marlow lied.

"I bet not, Marlow. Thing is, I don't fucking believe you," Learner said.

"I really don't give a fuck if you do or not, Tom. I just hate to think you are so consumed with hate for me that you would let an innocent kid suffer for it," Marlow replied

"Della, lock his ass up for assault and battery and breaking and entering," Chief Learner commanded. Della Martin sighed and slapped cuffs on Marlow. She put him in the back of her car and then climbed in to the driver's seat.

"Goddamit Marlow! Why the hell couldn't you keep your mouth shut for once?" Della demanded as she fired up the engine and put the car in gear.

"Tom is a fucking idiot. He'd rather that girl die than admit he was wrong," Marlow said from the back seat.

"I'm calling Walter so he can meet us at the station," Della said, removing her cell phone from her purse.

"I appreciate it, Della. Tell Walter I have evidence on my phone," Marlow told her.

"Dammit Marlow why did you have to tell me that?"

"Because Walter needs to know," Marlow replied. Even though he had smoked his limit for the day, he really wanted another cigarette.

Chapter Five

Walter Loomis was waiting at the Key West Police Department when Della Martin pulled into the parking lot. She recognized the car that belonged to Walter Loomis. "Your boss is here," Della called to Marlow as she rolled into the parking lot.

"Good to know," Marlow replied.

"Dammit, Ricky you do love to push things don't you?"

"I do," Marlow nodded.

"Why?" Walter asked.

"Because I can?" Marlow shrugged.

"I figured that much," Walter replied.

"I have pictures on my phone, Walter. Andrea was there," Marlow told him.

"Do you have his phone?" Walter looked at Della. She sighed loudly.

"I do," Della admitted.

"Do you know it contained evidence?"

"He told me," Della sighed.

"I need to see it," Walter told her.

"I'm sure you do," Della sighed.

"Then show it to me," Walter told her.

"Right," Della said, pulling out Marlow's phone and handing it to Walter.

The white-haired attorney pulled up the pictures. He looked them over. "Marlow is right, the girl was held at this address."

"I agree, but you want to tell Tom that?"

"Certainly. Tom has an issue with Marlow, he has for quite some time," Wally replied.

"I know that," Della nodded.

"He also has a problem with the relationship between the two of you," Walter told her.

"That is certainly a given," Della rolled her eyes.

"Then I will certainly let Tom know he is wrong, Della."

"I know you will, Walter."

"This is going to be a dirty case."

"I kinda figured that much."

"Good. That will save time later," Marlow told her.

On U.S. 1...

Andrea Gables opened her eyes. She wondered why Phil had sent her away. She thought she was making him happy. At least he had given her the shot before sending her away. Andrea smiled dreamily.

Andrea heard the voices of the men in the truck driving her north. Miami Phil had told her. So she could learn to do what his bosses wanted. One of the men was riding with her in the back of the van. He was dark-skinned with curly black hair and a thick black mustache.

"I am Tomas," he whispered, leaning over her.

"Hi Tomas," Andrea giggled. He kissed her neck and his mustache tickled. She giggled again.

"You like me?" Tomas asked.

"Of course. You're Phil's friend," Andrea smiled at him.

"Phil said you'd take care of me," Tomas said, his voice thicker somehow. His hands touched her legs, rubbing them. Andrea opened them and pulled up her gown, exposing a thatch of red hair.

"You like what you see, Tomas?" Andrea giggled.

"I like very much," Tomas told her as he unzipped his pants and lowered them. "Do you like this?" he whispered silkily.

"Very much," Andrea replied as she took him in her hand and guided him inside her...

Key West, Florida

"Ricky you have got to be more careful. You know Tom Learner hates your guts," Walter Loomis said.

"Tom is an asshole, Walter," Marlow shrugged. He really wanted another cigarette.

"You're fidgeting, Ricky."

"I know I am."

"You want to smoke?"

"I do."

"So why don't you?"

"I've had my five for the day."

"And you won't go past that?"

"No. That's what limits are for," Marlow sighed.

"To stay within?"

"Of course, Walter. Otherwise why have them?"

"Exactly. So it is a matter of personal discipline?"

"It is."

"We know Andrea Gables was in that house earlier. Where is she now?" Walter asked.

"That is a good question, Walter. She's in the pipeline, and I doubt if Phil is going to talk," Marlow said.

"I think that would be a reasonable assumption," Walter nodded.

"Me too," Marlow told him.

"So what then?"

"I think a trip to Miami might be in order," Marlow said.

"You think that is where that piece of shit sent her?" Walter asked, unable to contain his fury.

"I do Walter. There is more going on here than what we know."

"You seem sure of that?"

"I am. There is something off center about the father and his relationship with his daughter. Mom knows about it but isn't willing to talk. Even with her little girl missing, she's holding back. Why?" Marlow asked.

"Good question, Ricky. You believe that he was molesting her?"

"I think so. Mom knows but doesn't want to believe that her husband is more attracted to their daughter than her. So she stands up for the daughter, trying to get her out of her husband's reach," Marlow replied.

"And she fails. So she insists that he hire you to find the girl," Walter nodded.

"Revenge for what he had done, and to let him know that she knew," Marlow nodded.

"Families are strange, Ricky."

"Yes, Walter, they are," Marlow nodded

"And where does that leave the girl?" Walter asked.

"In the pipeline," Marlow sighed.

"Do you need my car or are you going to rent one?" Walter asked.

"Given what happened to the Pinto, Walter, I'll rent one," Marlow told him.

"Make sure you take the insurance," Walter said.

"Always," Marlow replied as he headed on foot to his place. The cops had his bike so he wasn't too worried about it for the moment. He would take a cab to the airport to rent a car to drive to Miami. He had no desire to see Walter's car blown up and he knew it was a possibility.

Marlow knew it would be morning before he started for Miami. He hoped that he managed a full night's sleep, but he was pretty sure that Chief Learner would certainly have other ideas about that, despite Walter's legal maneuvering. Still. Music still poured from the bars as Marlow walked down Duvall away from them.

He cut over a couple of blocks to Caroline and headed towards the cemetery. The farther away from Duval he moved, the more ominous the shadows seemed.

Marlow walked across an intersection and heard an engine start behind him. He didn't look back, writing it off as nerves. Then headlights came on and the engine noise accelerated. Marlow turned to see the car accelerating towards him, the headlights blinding him. He ran, sprinting across the street, hearing the squall of tires as they swerved to track him across the road. Marlow hit the fence on the run, grabbing it and propelling himself up and over it as the car hit the sidewalk and ran along it.

He hit the ground hard but rolled until he crashed into a tombstone with his back. Gasping for air, Marlow was up and running, dodging between headstones as bullets sought him in the darkness. He found a larger crypt and sought cover behind it. Sirens were drawing near and he heard the car speed off into the darkness.

Marlow stood and worked his way across to Fleming Street. The police were on the other side of the cemetery. Marlow flipped the fence and continued on his way. It was well after midnight when he reached his apartment. He unlocked the door and walked up the stairs. The lights revealed his Spartan apartment. Nobody was there but him. Learner had confiscated his .38, but Marlow immediately recovered his SCCY Centex 1 9mm auto from where he kept it concealed. The 9mm automatic had been a gift from Walter on his last case. Marlow kept the double-action only 9mm chamber loaded but he checked it nonetheless.

He didn't know who it was that had tried to run him down, but he was willing to bet that it had something to do with Phil Gordon and the case he was working on. Marlow held the pistol in hand as he checked his apartment and made sure it was clear.

Finally satisfied that he was alone, Marlow went into the kitchen and took a six-ounce crystal tumbler out of the cabinet and carried it to the fridge. He opened the freezer and pulled out a liter bottle of Skol vodka. He realized he could just as easily taken one of the bottles of Killian's Red from below, but the Vodka was what he felt he needed. He filled the tumbler half full and put the bottle back in the freezer.

Marlow walked over to the couch and sat down. He used the remote to tune in the old movie channel from

Miami. Key Largo was playing. Marlow enjoyed Bogart and Bacall. He took a slug of the vodka, feeling it burn down to his belly. Marlow took his phone from his pocket and put it on the coffee table.

Marlow took another drink and leaned back on the couch. It had been about a week since he had drank anything stronger than beer. He closed his eyes...

The snow swirled around them. Falling down from the black sky above. Marlow looked at the body on the floor of the alley. The normally black skin turned gray by the cold, the white flakes gathering on gray-white skin. Gino Fannaduchi looked up at him with cold dead eyes.

Marlow turned to face Nolan as he came up, his Maglite bright in Marlow's eyes. "I'm sorry, Marlow." Nolan told him. Three explosions. Three hammer-blows to his chest. Marlow fell to the ground. The snow continued to fall. He remembered the snowflakes touching his eyes. They covered them.

Marlow snapped awake, a cold sweat filming his skin. His hand found the butt of the pistol as his eyes scanned the darkness. The apartment house was quiet except for the white noise from the television. The station he had been watching had gone off the air. Marlow located the remote and turned the television off. The wind was blowing outside and he could hear it howling past the eaves.

From the sound of it a tropical storm was moving in and Marlow had not bothered to catch the earlier weather report to know if that was true. He sat up and picked up the 9mm autoloader from the coffee table and checked the apartment once more.

Once again he was the only one there. He put on Art Pepper's Winter Moon CD and went to his single bed and laid down on it. The pistol went on top of the nightstand and Marlow pulled a crisp white sheet up and over him and fell back into a deep sleep...

Chapter Six

Della Martin escorted Phil Gordon from the car into the Key West Police Department lock-up. His face had been bandaged from his encounter with Marlow in the bar. The suspect was sullen and pretty uncooperative, but she didn't care. He had molested the girl and she was underage. Della wanted nothing more than to give him a quick kick in the balls herself. However the bastard gave her no excuse. He went to his cell as docile as a little lamb.

Donny Osgood, the jailer grinned at her as she brought Gordon in. Donny was an old friend and they had even dated back in high school. Like her, he was a native born Conch.

"Keep this one isolated, Donny. He molested a young girl," Della told him. Donny frowned. His sister had been molested by a tourist. He stood and reached out and grabbed Gordon and force marched him to a cell. Della smiled. Gordon would be on every prisoner's radar before the sun rose and not in a good way.

Even the most hardened criminal looked at child molesters as bottom feeders, the lowest of the scum in the criminal pond. With that tag on him, Gordon would be branded within minutes if not hours with the most feared tag of the criminal underworld. And his days would be numbered, for everyone in the jail would be doing their best to figure out how to kill him...

Chief Tom Learner dropped into the chair behind his desk. He was beyond tired this night. The missing girl was rapidly becoming a nightmare for him. Phil Gordon had been on his radar for awhile, there had been several complaints against him. But when he tried to get the guy into court, the complaints had been dropped.

Learner had to wonder about that. Much as he hated to believe it, the odds were actually good that Marlow was right about this guy. But if he was, it only meant that Phil Gordon was the first stop in a pipeline of human trafficking.

Learner shook his head. It killed him to admit that Marlow was right about anything. Too many times the young private detective had made him look like a fool. That was neither something that Learner liked or appreciated.

Marlow awoke once more to the rising sun streaming in through his window. His mouth was dry and he grabbed for a bottle of water sitting next to the bed. He drained half of it in one long swallow. He rolled to a sitting position and put his feet on the floor.

It was not his most favorite time of day, but it was what it was. Marlow reached for his pack of cigarettes. He shook one out and stuck it into the corner of his mouth and then found the Bic lighter on the table next to where the pack of cigarettes had lasted. Marlow stroked the striker wheel with his thumb and a tongue of flame appeared. Marlow stuck the end of the cigarette into the flame.

He inhaled the flame through the paper tube filled with tobacco. Marlow exhaled smoke from his nostrils, looking like a legendary fire-breathing dragon as he did so. On shaky legs he stood and made his way to the bathroom.

He was almost done with the first cigarette of the day as he finished and flushed it away. He started the coffee maker and pulled on shorts and sneakers. Marlow stepped out of his apartment and headed for the beach. The morning run was a ritual he had began after starting work for Walter. He was up to almost half a mile now. The sun was climbing in the sky as Marlow started to run.

When he staggered back home, Marlow poured himself a cup of coffee before he hit the shower. By the time he was done it was cool enough to drink. Marlow dressed in cargo shorts and a pale green guayubera shirt. The SCCY 9mm was clipped in a holster inside his waistband since the Key West Police Department currently had his .38 in their custody. The two guns weighed about the same, though the automatic was thinner.

Marlow walked outside. He had left his bike on Stock Island, so he walked the few blocks to Harpoon Harry's where Ron greeted him and Marlow ordered his normal breakfast, two eggs over easy and two pieces of toast with butter and strawberry jam along with a cup of French vanilla roast.

"Looks good in here, Ron. So what was that mess in here all about?" Marlow asked, referring to an incident months before when the restaurant had been shot up by a bunch of crazy people.

"Just another one of Mick Murphy's misadventures. It happens again I'm going to make him start paying my insurance premiums," Ron shook his head.

"Well the French doors look nicer," Marlow told him as he finished his meal. He bought another cup of coffee in a to-go cup and walked outside. At 8 a.m. it was already eighty degrees but the breeze was pushing the humidity around made it feel slightly more comfortable.

Marlow hoped Della might be able to give him a ride to pick up his bike if it hadn't been impounded at the crime scene. He would need it to get out to the airport to rent a car for his trip to Miami.

"What has you out so early, Rick?" Dana Vincent called from across the street. Dana worked as a waitress at Sloppy Joes and she and Marlow had become friends.

"I need a ride. I ended up leaving my bike over on Stock Island last night. It was unexpected," Marlow told her.

"I bet," Dana rolled her eyes. "Case-related?"

"It was," Marlow said.

"Let's go. My pick-up is around the corner," Dana punched him lightly on the shoulder. "In return, you can thrill me with all the details you can't tell me about the case because of confidentiality.

Dana Vincent was a tall leggy redhead with blue eyes and freckles. She had curves in all the right places and in the sleeveless t-shirt she had knotted below her ample bosom and the daisy duke cut-offs, many people would have thought a threat to Marlow's relationship with Della. In that they would be wrong. Dana went the other way and she found Marlow and his escapades a wild source of amusement. Plus being a lesbian she was far more interested in Della than Marlow. But Marlow accepted her for who she was. Dana did the same for Marlow.

She had met a number of cops in her time, and not all of the experiences were pleasant ones. Marlow was different than most. Oh he had told his story one rainy night sitting and drinking after the bar had shut down. She had found him fascinating and they had become fast friends.

"Dana do you know anything about an asshole by the name of Phil Gordon? Marlow asked as they headed for her rusty Ford Ranger pick-up truck. Once it had been royal blue but exposure to salt air and sun had dimmed that luster and added rusty orange around the wheel wells.

"Feel good Phil. Your character assessment is dead on Marlow. He is an asshole," Dana confirmed.

"You know that personally? Or just hear it around?"

"Let's say that one night the bastard didn't want to take no for an answer until I dislocated his shoulder and sent his pig ass to the hospital," Dana shrugged.

"Was it you he didn't want to listen to no from?" Marlow's face looked like it was carved from stone.

"No my friend Carla. She's straight but had just been through a really bad break-up when she caught Phil's attention. Sonofabitch got her high, slipped something into her drink and then tried to take her home with him. I heard her tell him no that she wanted to go to the hospital. He told her she didn't need a hospital that he had some stuff at home that would make her feel better.

"I stepped in and took her out of his hands and the stupid bastard swung at me. Afterwards he couldn't wind-surf for about three months," Dana smiled at the memory. Marlow nodded.

"You know any other girls he pulled that shit with?" Marlow asked. He wanted a cigarette badly, but it was too soon.

"A few. Some are still around, some aren't." Dana shrugged.

"You know what happened to the ones that aren't?"

"Can't say I do," Dana shook her head.

"The ones that do, any idea why they never pressed charges?"

"Funny, no I don't," Dana shook her head slowly. They reached her truck and climbed inside.

"Can you check that out for me? He's involved in my current case," Marlow explained.

"Sure thing, Rick, just as soon as you tell me what this is all about," Dana replied pulling away from the curb. Marlow gave her the short version on the quick ride to Gordon's place on Stock Island. Marlow was amazed to find his Huffy in one piece and put it into the back of the truck.

"Kidnapping and white slavery. Sounds like that sick fuck," Dana shook her head as they headed back across the bridge to Key West.

"Bad part is I'm not sure he's the main problem," Marlow sighed.

"You mean the father?"

"I do. I'm not so sure putting this girl back with her parents is the right thing to do."

"What does Walter think?"

"I haven't asked him yet."

"Are you going to?"

"Eventually. After I find her," Marlow replied. He pulled his cigarettes out of his shirt pocket and shook one free. He stuck it in his mouth and replaced the pack in his pocket and then fished out his lighter and stroked the flame to life. Marlow touched the cigarette to the flame and drew it into the paper tube. Smoke shot from his nostrils.

"Rick, don't let this get personal," Dana told him.

"Dana, every case I work is personal. That's why I solve them," Marlow exhaled more smoke.

"So you tell me. I get a feeling this case is more than that."

"It isn't," Marlow told her. He knew he was lying to her. It went back to when he was a kid. There had been a girl, her name was Maggie. Like both Andrea and Dana she had red hair and freckles. Marlow had been 12 at the time. Maggie had been his best friend.

They played together often in the suburban neighborhood where Marlow had grown up. Suddenly Maggie had quit wanting to play. She had began to stay to herself, not wanting to talk or play with her friends. Marlow had mentioned it to his dad. One day Maggie just disappeared. Not long afterwards, her father was arrested.

A few days later, His dad had told him that Maggie wouldn't ever be back. Bad things had been done to her by bad people, one of which was her father. Marlow had cried for Maggie for a week. It was only now that he realized that Andrea Gables reminded him of Maggie. So yeah, this case was VERY personal. He vowed that he would find that poor young girl no matter what!

Dana dropped Marlow at Walter's and he locked his vintage Huffy in the rack. Then he stood and walked to the front door and entered the air-conditioned sanctuary that was Walter's office.

"Donuts in the conference room," Lola Ponsberry called as Marlow breezed by her to see Walter. Marlow waved at her and made it a point to stop in and grab a tiger-tail on his way to Walter's office. His cup of coffee was nearly empty as he munched the donut and dropped into the chair across from Walter Loomis.

"Anything new on the Gables case?" Walter looked up at him.

"Not so much yet. However I do have some very strong suspicions about what is going on and about Phil Gordon," Marlow replied.

"What do you mean?"

"Gordon is well known on the island and has a really bad reputation. I want to know why the cops have never moved on him," Marlow shrugged.

"That does seem like a prudent question," Walter nodded.

"Let's get it onto the record then. I'm going to call a cab to take me out to the airport to rent a car. Then I'm off to Miami," Marlow told his boss.

"Make sure you get receipts," Walter called after him.

Chapter Seven

Marlow made it a point to wheel his bike into the office before calling for a cab. He had also gone on-line and Googled Phil Gordon. He had also called KWPD and got a list of Gordon's known associates. Armed with that he walked to his apartment and packed a bag. From there he called for a taxi and when it pulled out headed for the airport.

Marlow studied the list of names and the addresses that went with them. There were four in Miami that held potential, the rest were on Stock Island or other close by islands. He would check on them later. His gut was telling him that Andrea had been sent to Miami. The question was why?

Did they intend to put her on the streets as a prostitute? Or to mule drugs for them? Or maybe something even worse. Down on Key West Marlow had heard that there were snuff films being made in the Keys. He closed his eyes and let his head fall back. He had moved to Key West to escape the dark serious shit he had experienced back in New York.

It just went to prove that people were animals no matter where you lived, from the Big Apple to Paradise. Marlow shook his head. He pulled the bill of his white Corona baseball cap lower to shield his face. His eyes were covered by his dark lensed sunglasses.

Walter was working on getting his revolver back from KWPD so for this trip he was carrying the SCCY 9mm that Walter had given him. He had a Browning Hi-Power packed away in his suitcase as well. The taxi reached the airport and Marlow gave Nick Randall a five-dollar tip over the fare. Nick was a good guy and had a wife and a houseful of kids to support on his salary as a taxi driver. He also worked as a bouncer at the Green Parrot on weekends.

The girl at the rental counter rolled her eyes when Marlow wrote his name on the rental application. "You want the insurance?" she asked. Her nametag read Patty and she had brown hair with blonde highlights. She also looked to barely be in her twenties.

"Of course I do, Patty," Marlow replied.

"I heard about you," Patty snapped her gum.

"What did you hear?" Marlow asked with a hint of amusement.

"You get cars blown up and shot up," she snapped her gum again.

"So young and so cynical," Marlow grinned. He counted cash out onto the white counter.

"Here you go," she slid keys across the counter to him. Ford Focus. Marlow nodded. A good car but not as good as his Pinto had been. Marlow scooped up the keys and took his receipt and headed for the door.

Sweat beaded on his skin when he stepped back out into the heat. When he reached the car he immediately rolled down the windows in the front seat. He fired up the engine and fastened the seatbelt. He tuned the radio to the

Miami Jazz station as he put it in gear and headed out of the parking lot...

Dana Vincent headed for the beach, her conversation with Marlow sticking with her. Phil Gordon had always been a sleaze, but she had not expected what Marlow had told her. She had plenty of friends that Gordon had hurt. Maybe now that he was in jail, there might be a way to get payback for them. Dana smiled. It wasn't a pleasant one as she headed for the Schooner which still maintained pay phones...

"Marlow, where are you?" Della Martin's voice filled his ear when he answered his phone.

"On my way to Miami, why?" Marlow asked.

"The Chief isn't going to be happy about that," Della sighed.

"Tell him to take it up with Walter. That may quiet him down," Marlow replied.

"When were you going to tell me you were heading for Miami?" Della asked.

"I thought I just did," Marlow replied.

"Rick."

"Don't start with that crap Della. I have a job to do just like you. Only I go where the case takes me. I don't have the same rules you do," Marlow told her.

"I know and you play fast and loose with the ones you have. Dammit Rick, from everything I've been able to find out about Gordon, he's bad news and so are the people he hangs with!" Della snapped.

"Phil Gordon is no longer important to me, Della. Finding the girl is."

"Marlow, what I'm saying is that Phil Gordon is not someone you want to have coming along behind you."

"If he does, I'll deal with him Della. I've dealt with worse," Marlow said reminding her of his most recent case where he had solved his own shooting which had taken place back in New York City.

"Marlow, this Gordon is a total bottom feeder. He makes those people look like amateurs. He's been linked to some heavy hitters in the drug trade here," Della said.

"Half that damned island is involved with heavy hitters in the drug trade, or at least they used to be. You know that as well as I do," Marlow shook his head as he drove.

"Not like Gordon. He's connected. In fact a high priced lawyer from Miami just walked through the doors with a writ of Habeas Corpus to get him out of jail," Della whispered.

"That is very interesting. Thanks for the heads up, Della. I gotta go," Marlow broke the connection. This was a new wrinkle. He dialed Walter's number.

"Loomis Law Practice," Lola Ponsberry answered. Lola was a handsome woman approaching sixty but who loved her Octogenarian boss with all her heart. Walter was only starting to show some interest, despite what he referred to as their "shameful" age difference.

"Lola, can you put me through to Walter?" Marlow asked.

"Certainly. Please hold," Lola said. A moment later Walter's voice came on the line.

"Ricky my boy, what do you need?" Walter Loomis asked.

"Della just called to say that a high-powered Miami attorney had arrived to get Phil Gordon out of jail. Can you find out his name?" Marlow asked.

"I can. Give me half an hour and I'll call you back," Walter broke the connection. Marlow grinned. That name might well help him nail down who to talk to in Miami.

"Lola, I'm heading over to the Police Station. Please reschedule any appointments," Walter told her as he headed for the door. A taxi pulled up front as Walter reached the curb and he climbed inside. He gave the driver the address of the police station and settled back in the seat, his briefcase clutched on his lap.

This particular case had caught his attention. He wasn't exactly sure why, but it had. It might have something to do with his estrangement from his own daughters, it might be something else all together. Walter couldn't say for sure. But with each revelation, he was being drawn deeper into it just as Marlow was.

Walter wished he knew why Marlow was so drawn to it. But so far he had no clue. Ricky was an incredibly self-contained person. Autonomous was a good word to describe him. Marlow was not one to let too many people get too close to him. That he had let Della get as close as she had was a wonder that Walter found no less than amazing.

Of course Marlow had been working with Dr. Jessica Harmon on his PTSD and that could well be a big part of it. Walter had recommended the psychiatrist, as had Della

Martin, but it had taken an order from an ER physician and a threat of jail to get Marlow to start seeing her.

At any rate it seemed to be helping Marlow, and that was the least that Walter had hoped for.

Phil Gordon squinted at the bright sunlight as he walked out of the Key West Police Station. He looked at Frances Bertram, the lawyer that had bailed him out. Gordon knew that Bertram worked for the Escobar brothers. Bertram had made other things go away when needed. The Escobar's knew what a valuable resource Phil was. He did a lot of shit for them. "You got my sunglasses?" he asked Bertram.

"Were you wearing them when you were arrested?" Bertram sighed.

"No. It was dark out," Phil shook his head.

"Then why would I have them. Mr. Escobar sent a message. Lay low and keep out of sight for a few days until this blows over. Understand?"

"Sure thing. Tell Mr. Escobar I said thank you."

"Sure thing, Phil," the attorney spat his name like it was a curse. Then he turned and walked away leaving Gordon standing there on the street. Phil Gordon frowned at the attorney's back before walking across the street to a shop where he could buy a pair of sunglasses.

Frankie Tomlinson who worked in the t-shirt shop gave Gordon a funny look when he walked through the door. Frankie was a body builder and was a black belt in kung fu. "I need some sunglasses, Frank," Gordon said.

"Get out of my shop. Your money won't buy anything here," Frankie replied coldly.

Phil Gordon bristled. "My money is good anywhere on this fucking island!"

"Not anymore, Asshole. You'd do well to leave the Keys in general, baby raper!"

"What the fuck are you talking about Frank?'

"You kidnapping and raping little beach girls. Underage ones like that red head. Get out of my shop before I break your neck," Frankie hissed between clenched teeth, his eyes narrowed with rage. He dragged a Louisville Slugger from behind the counter.

"Okay, I'm going," Phil stumbled backwards out into the street and the blinding sunshine. "But I'll be back later on," he mumbled. Frankie watched him walk away and then dug his cell phone out of his pocket. He dialed a number.

"Fucking bastard was just in here but I ran him out. Phil Gordon ain't welcome no place on Key West," Frankie said. Dana had talked to him earlier and now the story was moving along the Coconut Telegraph about Phil Gordon. In Frankie's opinion, the guy should have been run out of town a long damn time ago!

By the time he picked up his truck and drove back to Stock Island, Phil Gordon had a knot growing in his stomach. Something was going down, something bad. Every place he stopped on Key West he had been met with threats and hostility. People who had at least been polite before now openly glared at him with hate in their eyes.

What had that asshole at the t-shirt shop said? About him kidnapping and raping the red head? He had to be talking about Andy. Gordon figured it was that damn lady cop. She had to have put the word out. Well, she was gonna pay for that. He'd make sure of it! She wasn't too bad looking and it might be a whole lot of fun for him. Phil grinned as he climbed out of his truck and walked towards the dilapidated shack he called home.

"You don't want to go in there," a voice called from the porch next door. Gordon looked over and spotted an old Negro with fuzzy white hair and a fuzzy white beard. He knew the man as Donny.

"Why not Donny?"

"They was some right unfriendly looking folks here earlier. I suspect they left you a surprise you might not want to walk in on," Donny replied.

Phil stepped off the porch and walked over to Donny's house. "What did they look like?"

"Like a bunch of angry folks from across the bridge. You get into some kind of trouble over there?" Donny asked.

"Maybe I did," Phil said thoughtfully.

"I though as much," Donny nodded.

"Why did you tell me, Donny?"

"You been a good neighbor to me. Not too loud and you don't ask questions. Plus you ain't got no damn dogs that come out and shit in my yard. I liked that about you," Donny shrugged.

"Donny, I want you to go inside. I think I'm gonna throw a rock at my front door and I don't want you to get hurt," Phil told him.

"I can do that. If you end up needing a place to sleep tonight, my couch will hold you," Donny said as he turned and walked inside his house. Phil walked down and picked up a rock. He walked out to the end of his driveway. He had been a fairly good pitcher when he played ball back in high school. He wound up and threw it at his front door. The Rock hit the door and the shack exploded in a ball of fire.

Phil Gordon was knocked down on the street by the concussion of the blast. He looked at Donny's house. The old Negro was looking at him.

"I guess this means you'll be needing a place to stay," he cackled.

Chapter Eight

Frances Bertram pulled the number up from his contact list and dialed it. It rang three times before it was answered on the other end and a voice he knew all too well spoke. "Report," it commanded.

"Gordon is out on bail but I think he is becoming a liability," Bertram said.

"How so?" asked the voice on the other end.

"He's far too arrogant. He thinks you need him more than he needs you."

"Why do you say that?"

"He didn't even ask what he was charged with. Key West is a small island and word travels fast. The people are ready to tar and feather him and run him out of town on a rail. Gordon is too stupid to realize it," Bertram said.

"Then perhaps the populace will take care of him without us needing to do anything," the voice replied.

"Perhaps. However, I still think he's a loose cannon," Bertram said before the connection was broken. Bertram shook his head. Perhaps it was time to retire.

Key West, Florida

Walter Loomis looked across the desk at Della Martin. "Do you have the attorney's name?"

Della was wearing a lime green skirt and top with a corral jacket and a pooka shell necklace. Her long dark hair was held back in a ponytail.

"His name was Frances Bertram," Della replied.

"Do you know who retained him?" Walter asked.

"I ran a check on his clientele," Della nodded.

"And?"

"The Escobar brothers are his only clients. Outside of Phil Gordon," Della sighed.

"So then it would be a good bet that Gordon also works for the Escobar brothers," Walter said.

"I would say so, yes," Della told him.

"Walter, where the hell is Marlow?" Tom Learner asked from the doorway.

"On his way to Miami in pursuit of a case," Walter replied.

"I told him not to leave town," Tom growled red faced.

"And he has a job to do," Walter replied.

"He assaulted Phil Gordon."

"Who he proved to be a child molester. Are you in the business of protecting Child Molesters, Tom? Maybe I should call Thom Hark over at the citizen. You know he is now a feature reporter for them since the Solares Hill bit the dust?"

"Walter."

"Do you really want to fight me on this Tom? It is an election year after all," Walter looked at him.

"Goddam you Walter!" Tom howled.

"One more word..." Walter let it hang.

"I fucking give up!" Tom Learner threw his hands in the air and walked away.

"You know how to play him," Della chuckled.

"Like a piano," Walter chuckled.

"Are you going to pass this on to Rick?"

"I am. It may narrow down his search in Miami," Walter replied.

Deputy Larry Harris looked at the remains of Phil Gordon's shack. The fire department hadn't got there quickly enough to save anything. Harris was pretty sure they hadn't tried. Word was spreading pretty fast up and down the Keys on the Coconut Telegraph about Phil Gordon and the shit he was into.

"Are you gonna do something about this or not?" Gordon demanded angrily.

"I'll look into it, Phil. But if I were you, I'd take it as a sign you aren't exactly welcome around here anymore," Harris replied.

"You think?" Gordon shook his head.

"Nobody wants child molesters in their neighborhood, Phil," Harris said, a hard edge to his voice.

"Fuck you then. Nobody is running me out!" Gordon snarled.

"You got a home to go to? Seems to me they already have," Harris smiled, then he turned and walked to his car leaving Gordon standing at the side of the road.

"Told you it was gonna go like that," Donny said.

"Yes you did. What do you know, Donny?" Gordon asked.

"I heard the rumors, and I've seen the young girls that have gone in and out of your place. But like I said, you been a good neighbor to me," Donny shrugged.

"I appreciate that," Gordon sighed.

"Son, you stay around they ain't gonna keep missing. You need to think about that," Donny told him.

"I'm gonna get some payback for this shit. If the law won't do anything, I'll do it myself," Gordon snarled.

"Be careful that getting the payback don't get you killed," Donny said.

Marlow kept the windows of the rented Ford Focus down as he drove up Highway 1 towards Miami. The radio was tuned to the Miami Jazz station and Coltrane was doing his thing as Marlow smoked his third cigarette of the day.

His cell phone rang and he snatched it up off the seat. It was Walter. Marlow answered it as he rolled up the window. "What have you got for me, Walter?" Marlow asked.

"A name. Frances Bertram, attorney at law. His only clients include Phil Gordon and the Escobar brothers from Miami," Walter said.

"Interesting information," Marlow said.

"It should help narrow down your search."

"It should. I'm gonna check in with Parker and see what he can tell me."

"Probably a good idea. Locals are a wealth of information," Walter nodded.

"They certainly can be, especially when they are cops," Marlow agreed.

Captain Dave Parker walked outside the Miami Dade Police Station. He stopped and pulled out a cigar fired it up. Today he was wearing a white tropical weight suit over a pale green shirt and a slightly darker green tie. Brown wing tips covered his feet. A Glock 20 hung under his left arm. His cell phone buzzed letting him know he had a call. Parker saw who the call was from and answered it. "Rick Marlow to what do I owe the pleasure?" Parker asked.

"I'm heading your way on a case. A missing girl, started out as a runaway but now seems to be turning into something else," Marlow replied.

"Lots of runaways in Miami, Marlow."

"I know. But how any of them were hauled off in a truck belonging to the Escobar brothers after being forcibly hooked on drugs?"

"Probably more than I know about but you have my interest now."

"I thought I might. You know the Escobar's then?"

"I do."

"You know they got a mouth-piece named Frances Bertram?" Marlow asked.

"I've heard the name," Parker acknowledged.

"They also have some local muscle on Key West, a jackass named Phil Gordon. Seems he scouts out vulnerable young girls, feeds them a fast line, gets them hooked and sends them to Miami. Some come back, some get busted hauling product but they don't know who for."

"Sounds like the Escobar Brothers all right. You sure the girl was headed this way?" Parker asked.

"I am," Marlow replied.

"Call me back when you get to town. I may have something for you by then," Parker broke the connection and dropped the phone back into his coat pocket. He blew out a thick cloud of smoke. The Escobar Brothers. Parker smiled. He had been after them for a few years. Marlow might just be the catalyst for the perfect storm.

Phil Gordon sat on Donny's sofa drinking a beer. There wasn't a whole lot he could do about his current situation in daylight, but once the sun went down it would be a different story. Frankie would be the first to feel his wrath. He was gonna burn that damn t-shirt shop to the ground. After that, he was gonna look up that Lady Detective and teach her a thing or two!

Simon Escobar sipped from the wine glass as he regarded his brother Gomez who sat across from him smoking a fat Cuban cigar. "Do you really think this is a wise idea?" Simon had thinning black hair filled with streaks of white that was slicked back on his head with a thick pomade that smelled slightly of coconut and lemon. A Pencil thin mustache covered his lip. He smoked a cigarette in a thin holder of the type reminiscent of a 1940's movie.

"I think it is a delightful idea. Using Harold Gables' daughter to mule our drugs down from Miami. I have him on film already sexually abusing her while her mother does nothing. Harold doesn't know it, but he will do anything we tell him to do," Gomez Escobar laughed.

"I am not so sure. Bertram feels that Gordon is becoming a liability. I agree with him," Simon blew out smoke rings.

"Then eliminate him. We can always find someone to replace him."

"Bertram seems to think the locals might well take care of that for us. Word of his predilections has gotten out and has spread through the lower Keys. He should be shot," Simon shook his head.

"He would not be the first," Gomez shrugged.

"Nor the last," Simon sighed.

"If he survives until morning put a contract out on him. I will find a replacement soon enough," Gomez waved his arms dismissively. Simon frowned at his older brother. Gomez was getting too caught up in his own fantasy of their lives. Gomez was thin, but with a thick head of curly dark hair with dark brown eyes and a quick smile. His cheekbones were high and his nose was long and aristocratic. A well-trimmed goatee covered his chin.

"I think you are making a mistake, Brother. I think we should be laying low right now. I think mucho trouble is headed our way," Simon said.

"Trouble is something we will meet head on, Brother. Don't worry about it," Gomez laughed.

Simon ignored his brother's prediction. His gut was telling him that Danger was on the way and that there was no way around it!

"Hey Della, how is it going?" Patrolwoman Ashley Gordon called from her car across the street.

"Fair to middling," Della replied.

"Glad to hear it," Ashley replied with a grin.

"You any relation to Phil Gordon?" Della asked nervously.

"Not that I know of," Ashley smiled.

"Be thankful," Della told her.

"I am, Sarge. Believe me I am."

"Glad to hear it Ashley."

"I've been hearing things, Della."

"Most of the island has. Seems like the Coconut Telegraph had kicked into over-drive on this one." Della sighed.

"You gotta admit there was certainly good reason," Ashley said.

"Not if it causes trouble in the streets. This time it might," Della said,

"He's going to be trouble isn't he? And not just for your boyfriend?" Ashley asked.

"Yeah, I think so. I also think the stupid bastard doesn't realize how much danger he's in," Della sighed.

"Why do you say that?" Ashley looked at her.

"Think about it Ashley. All the rape and brutality charges against him that were suddenly dropped. All of a sudden nobody is afraid any more. How many of them will be looking for payback? How many will be looking to get even? I think there is a damn good chance if Phil Gordon sticks around he's going to end up dead," Della said.

Chapter Nine

Miami, Florida

Rick Marlow dropped his suitcase on the bed of the motel that Lola had gotten him a reservation for. He lit his third cigarette of the day and took a moment just to enjoy the taste of the smoke as he drew it in and let it out. Smoking rooms were getting harder to find. Marlow pulled a bottle out of the suitcase and unscrewed the cap and he used it to fill one of the six-ounce tumblers provided by the hotel. Marlow added some ice cubes and took a sip. The vodka tasted good as it burnt its way down to his belly.

Andy Gables was out there somewhere. Going through God alone knew what. Sure, he knew she wasn't Maggie but she sure reminded him of her. It was likely a silly thing, but one that he held on to. Maggie had been his friend. He had in his own way loved her. But they were kids. And then she was gone and he was left feeling hollow and empty.

Even his dad had been little help after Maggie had disappeared. His father had refused to tell him anything more about Maggie and Marlow had resented him for that fact ever after.

Marlow was not going to let Andy Gables disappear like Maggie had. He would bring Andy back no matter who he had to kill to do so. He hoped that both Della and Walter would understand that. Marlow took another sip of the vodka and ice.

Andy Gables stretched languidly as she rolled to her feet. Tomas had been an excellent lover. She was hungry and wanted something to eat. She hoped that Tomas was going to bring her something. She walked around the room where she had been left. There was a knock at the door.

Andy walked over to the door and opened it. A man stood there. A well dressed man with slicked-back hair and a pencil thin mustache. He stepped inside. "Hello, Andrea," he said.

Key West, Florida

Night was falling over the island. Phil Gordon left his truck on Stock Island and walked back over the bridge. It would be better that nobody knew he was back until he had done what he came to do and then left again. They would have no problem figuring it out when he was gone.

He would like to start with that goddamn Marlow, but he heard he had took off chasing after fucking Andy like the bitch even mattered. She was just another split-tail mule. He couldn't figure out why Gomez Escobar was even so interested in her. Gordon kept to the shadows as he walked. Word had gotten around about him.

Nobody respected him anymore. Now they all thought he was lower than dog shit. Well that was gonna change soon enough. He was about to get some payback tonight. Gordon chugged at the can of Pabst Blue Ribbon that Donny had given him. He was sweating from the walk, even at night the temperature hadn't fallen below 80 degrees.

Gordon used the can to wipe sweat from his brow as he joined the crowds on Duval Street. Once in the crowd he was just another anonymous partier in the night. He studiously avoided his regular hangouts and instead made his way to Frankie's t-shirt shop. Fucking body builder thought he was a big man with his baseball bat.

Gordon slipped behind the small shop that fronted on Duval. There was still light coming from the back door. Gordon smiled. The angels were fucking smiling down on him. He drained the beer can and set it down. Gordon tried the knob. It turned easily under his hand. He opened the door and slipped silently inside.

A radio was playing a Beach Boys tune about a hot-rodding old lady in Pasadena as Gordon by-passed the office to reach the front counter. Frankie was in the small office totaling the day's take. Gordon found the Louisville slugger. He hefted the bat and gave it a couple of practice swings. It felt good. Whistling soundlessly Gordon stepped into the office and hefted the bat to his shoulder. "Hey Frankie fuck up," he said and swung the bat.

Frankie fell back, blood spattering from his face. "Am I fucking welcome now?" Gordon swung the bat again and again. Frankie lay on the floor in a pool of blood. Gordon was gasping for air from his efforts. He wasn't done yet. He tossed a bunch of papers from the desk onto Frankie's body. Gordon pulled a book of matches from his pocket. He pulled one out and struck it to life and dropped it on the papers atop Frankie. The papers caught flame. He started fires in other areas and the flames caught the shirts on fire and then things really got going. Gordon was laughing as he walked out the back door, the inside of the shop engulfed in flames.

Della Martin was off duty and sitting in The Keys Piano Bar. Michael Thomas was tickling the ivories and she was sipping a cosmopolitan as she listened. He was doing a soulful rendition of "As Time Goes By" and it made her think of Marlow. She wondered how he was doing up in Miami. It surprised her that she missed him as much as she did. She knew he had strong feelings for her, but she still questioned her own feelings.

Marlow had been through a lot, more than most men and not all of it was good. He carried a lot of emotional and mental baggage. She wasn't a hundred percent sure she wanted to climb aboard that particular train. Sure, she was dealing with her own baggage, but was she really ready to take on his as well? She would have to discuss that with Dr. Harmon. Della took another sip of her drink. Then she heard the sound of sirens and headed for the door.

Della watched two fire trucks roar past heading towards Mallory Square. She pushed out the door and hurried after the fire-trucks. Tom Learner and Mike McCoy were already on the scene when Della arrived. The small storefront was engulfed in flames.

"This looks bad," McCoy said.

"Anybody got a hold of Frankie?" Della asked.

"We think he might be inside," Tom Learner told her.

"Well shit," Della sighed. She had liked Frankie. He was a good guy.

"With Marlow being out of town I know he had nothing to do with it," Chief Learner said casually.

"Why do you go out of your way to be an asshole, Chief?" Della looked at him.

"It gives me something to do," Learner replied nastily.

"Any ideas who might have done this?" McCoy asked.

"Not off hand," Della shook her head.

"Somebody does," Learner said.

"I'd guess so," McCoy agreed.

"I'll ask around," Della said.

"Thanks," McCoy told her.

"This isn't over," Tom Learner predicted.

"No, I suspect it isn't," Della agreed.

Phil Gordon watched from the shadows. He had been surprised to see the lady cop walk up on the scene. She didn't seem the type, but then you never knew. He waited. When she left, he would follow her...

Miami, Florida

Marlow sat in his rental car eating a ham and cheese sandwich he had purchased at a nearby convenience store. He washed the last bite down with a swallow of Code Red Mountain Dew. He was sitting outside the office building where the Escobar Brothers based their business. Walter had called him and given him an address. He was still waiting to hear back from Dave Parker.

Marlow had dialed in a local Miami Salsa station. He was becoming more interested in Latin Jazz and enjoyed listening to it almost as he did the likes of Art Pepper and

John Coltrane. He thought about another cigarette and decided to wait until he had finished the sandwich. He had a bag of Chips Ahoy chocolate chip cookies for dessert.

Marlow realized that it was highly unlikely that the Escobars would have Andrea in the office complex, but it was something to check out. Walter and Dave Parker were trying to track down other properties belonging to the Cuban brothers. Places where the likelihood of finding Andrea Gables would be more likely.

For now however, the office was all he had. The sun was going down and people were leaving the building. Not that that meant much. He had no idea what either of the Escobar brothers looked like. Marlow was working blind at the moment and he didn't like it at all. He finished the sandwich and washed it down with a swallow of Code Red. He eyed the bag of cookies. He opened it and took one out, biting into it. They were the chewy soft kind and he enjoyed the taste. He took another swallow of Code Red.

Finally he took out his pack of cigarettes and shook one free. This was number four for the day. He pulled out his lighter and lit it. He knew that the Escobar Brothers had a suite of offices on the fourth floor. He wondered about the security in the building. He figured they were probably uniformed rent-a-cops, but they might be a little better than that.

Marlow exhaled a cloud of smoke and drew in more, the cherry on the end of the cigarette flaring to life. He considered what he was going to do, and then pulled out his phone and dialed Dave Parker's number. He was pretty sure that the Miami-Dade detective was not going to be especially happy with him.

"Parker," the detective answered.

"Marlow. What can you tell me about the security at the Escobar Brothers office complex?"

"Why do you want to know?"

"Curiosity?"

"What are you planning, Marlow?" Parker asked.

"You may not want to know," Marlow told him.

"I'm pretty sure I don't," Parker sighed.

"So are you going to answer the question?"

"Might take some time."

"Not like I have anywhere else to be," Marlow flicked the cigarette out the window.

"I'll call you back."

"I'll be here," Marlow broke the connection. He grabbed another chocolate chip cookie and nibbled at it. Perhaps with Parker's help he wouldn't need to burgle the office, but it might be fun.

Simon Escobar looked down at the bed. Andrea Gables whimpered under his gaze. Her lips were puffy and bleeding. "You did well. Next time you will do better," he told her, his voice as oily as an eel sliding over her flesh. He had already dressed. "Now you know what I like, next time you will try harder to please me. Phillip said you were eager to please," he told her, smiling. Her left cheek was puffy and the eye was swelling shut and blackening.

Andrea whimpered again, struggling to cover herself with the sheet. Her body was bruised from where he had beaten her. Pain fogged her brain. Simon took a small case from his jacket pocket and removed a syringe from it. He stabbed the needle into her arm and depressed it, then withdrew it and put it back into its case. Andrea felt herself began to float, a white fog surrounding her senses. The pain went away and she was floating once more...

Key West, Florida

Della Martin headed back down Duval Street towards her car. The Key West Bar was only a couple of blocks away. She was away from the worst of the crowds. She stopped for a moment to take a breath. Frankie had been a good guy, a friend even. Della looked over her shoulder and that was when she saw him.

A man, who seemed to be following her, but who stayed back in the shadows. Was this the guy that had set Frankie's shop on fire? Or just a run of the mill predator that had chosen the wrong prey? Either way, she was about to find out. Della drew her service pistol from her purse and spun around to face him. The man vanished into the shadows.

Della frowned. She had a bad feeling about the man. That was a given. Part of her wished that Marlow had not gone to Miami. He might be an asshole sometimes, but he was her asshole and that made it okay.

Chapter Ten

Phil Gordon took a deep breath and let it out slowly. That has been close. Thankfully he had been standing at a spot where he could slip into an alley and hide in the shadows, though it galled him to do so. But even he realized that facing her with her holding a gun was purely foolish!

The lady cop would have to wait for another time. But there were a couple of others he had recognized from Donny's description of the people that had set the bomb in his house. One guy lived in the Bight on a small sailing boat. The boat would sink before morning. Preferably with the son of a bitch inside it!

He had taken great delight in beating Frankie to death with the ball bat. He had always hated the superior way the guy acted, flashing his goddamn muscles around like he was king shit on the beach and in his fucking t-shirt shop. It had even made him a little horny. With any luck he could take care of that tonight, though not with the lady cop like he had planned. Maybe he would pick some stranger, a tourist girl later who had no idea who he was. Phil nodded to himself. That was sounding more and more like a plan.

Della made her way to her car, unlocked it and climbed inside without ever taking her hand off of her gun. She locked the doors before she even started the car and only then did she release her grip on the gun. The guy in the shadows had looked familiar, but she couldn't place him. Her heart was pounding in her chest.

Della tried to calm her breathing as she broke into huge sobs. Hot tears gushed down her cheeks. Della laid her head on the steering wheel while she fought for control. Her hands were shaking as was her entire body. It was, she knew, a manifestation of the PTSD from when she had been shot and the feelings of absolute helplessness that had come from that.

It took several minutes to regain control. After that she pulled out her phone and dialed Dr. Harmon. Speaking slowly and hesitantly she left a message for the doctor to call her and then Della broke the connection. Della started the car and drove back to her home. Once inside she bolted the door. Della found a bottle of whiskey and a tumbler and filled it to the brim. She didn't bother adding ice as she chugged half the six-ounce tumbler. It burned all the way down, but when it hit her stomach, the heat flowed outwards through her body.

Della took a long drink and then drained the tumbler. This time she only filled it half-full as she felt the alcohol racing through her system. She put some Benny Carter on the CD player and sat in the dark. Her gun on the table beside her chair and drank some more...

Miami, Florida

Marlow had put on a cheap windbreaker and gotten a box from a dumpster. He bought tape at the convenience store and taped it shut after adding some pieces of brick and newspaper. He addressed it to the Escobar Brothers and put the building's address on it. He had also purchased a clipboard and legal pad and a pen.

It was full dark now. He got out of his car carrying the box and clipboard and knocked on the front door of the building. A bored looking security guard got up and walked to the door. "Waddya want?" the guard yelled through the glass.

"Got a delivery here for Mr. Escobar," Marlow yelled back.

"Just a minute," said the guard as he turned and walked back to his desk and fished the door key out of a drawer. Apparently after hours deliveries for the Escobar Brothers were not unusual. It was a fact he made note of.

Marlow waited, trying to look bored. Finally the guard returned and unlocked the door. "I need you to sign for it. First stop of the night," Marlow smiled and shook his head. He had written Escobar's name on the tablet and the address and drew a line for a signature.

"Sure thing, Pal. Happens all the time," the guard replied. Marlow noted that his name was T. Thompson. He reminded Marlow a bit of George Carlin, a recently deceased comedian.

"Sign right here," Marlow held out the clipboard and pen. The package was on the desk. The guard took both and then Marlow hit him with a right cross that dropped him like a pole-axed steer. Marlow took the man's belt and used it to bind his hands behind his back, and then he found the keys to all the offices and climbed into the elevator and rode it up to the floor with their offices.

The office was walnut paneled and looked like it was a man's world. The Machismo was so thick you could cut it with a knife and there was no on-site security to speak off. It took less than a minute for Marlow to come up with a list of their property holdings and print it out. He grabbed the pages and folded them up and stuffed them in his pocket.

Marlow made a quick exit, grabbing both the box and the clipboard on his way out. He had what he had come for. Marlow tossed the box into the back seat and climbed into the driver's seat. He drove back to his motel and went to his room. Once there he poured himself another cup of vodka and added some Mt. Dew.

He realized that some would consider him as low class for using Mt. Dew as a mixer. Marlow didn't really care. His cell phone rang. Marlow looked at it. Dave Parker. Marlow answered.

"Hey Dave, what have you got?" Marlow asked.

"I got your ass on a silver platter if I wanted it," Parker replied.

"I figured you would," Marlow replied.

"They had fucking security cameras."

"Which you will quash because you are on the side of justice and want to see Escobar locked up."

"There is that," Parker agreed.

"You make it seem like there is any other outcome?"

"There could be," Parker said.

Marlow awoke with a headache. He had fallen off the wagon in a major way the night before. How much of it was the case and how much of it was because he wanted to? It was something he would discuss with Dr. Harmon at their next session. He stumbled his way to the bathroom and took care of his morning ablutions and came out. There was a small coffee maker and he put it into service.

While the coffee perked, Marlow shaved and took a shower. He felt slightly more human as he walked out with the hotel towel cinched around his waist. His surgery scars stood out lividly against his pale white flesh. Marlow poured himself a cup of coffee and added sweetener.

He stirred it in and took a sip. It tasted good despite being motel coffee. Marlow sighed. He carried the coffee to the nightstand and got dressed in baggy cargo shorts and a sleeveless muscle shirt. He clipped the SCCY 9mm to his waistband and pulled on an aloha shirt to cover it.

Marlow headed out the door. He had the list he had printed out the night before from the offices of the Escobar brothers. He had elected to leave the car behind and took a taxi to the first address.

It was a strip mall and open for business. Marlow crossed it off his list as he gave the driver the next address....

Della puked into the toilet. She had drunk far too much the night before after returning home. Now it was her turn to worship on the alter of the porcelain god. She had managed to keep the vomitus out of her long dark hair and had staggered into an icy cold shower. She emerged from the shower feeling much better than when she had entered it. She vigorously toweled herself off and dressed.

Today she wore a lime green pantsuit with a coral top, with coral heels. A shell necklace hung around her neck. Della walked down to her car. She approached it with caution and made sure that no one lurked inside before entering it herself.

Della started the motor and put the car in gear and drove to the police station. She parked in her accustomed place in the parking lot. A Cold chill was in the air, courtesy of a freak storm that had come out of the north.

Della had considered pulling on her winter coat before leaving that morning, but she had not really believed that the cold snap would reach so far south as to affect Key West. Della drove to Harpoon Harry's for breakfast. It was one of Marlow's favorite eateries and Lou the owner met her and seated her. Seconds later she had a steaming coffee in front of her. "Did you order this weather?" Lou asked.

"Not me, Lou. I can't stand the cold. Must have been Marlow before he went to Miami," Della replied

"I wondered, he's usually in here by now."

"Chasing a runaway. Any news about the fire last night?"

"They found Frankie inside."

"Shit, I was afraid they might."

"Chief Fraga said it looked like arson," Lou told her.

"That's terrible! Why would someone want to do that?" Della shook her head as she sipped at her coffee. She ordered eggs and toast, not sure her stomach would tolerate more than that this morning. Once she finished she paid her bill and drove to the department.

Chief Learner didn't look like he had managed to get any sleep at all. He looked up bleary eyed as she walked in to his office. "Frankie Goldman is dead. Doc said he was beaten to death and was dead before the place burned," Learner told her.

"Who's working it?" Della asked.

"Quintana and Gray. Della, I've been hearing a lot of shit on the street about Phil Gordon being a child molester and his house was blown up yesterday. Ask around see what you can find out about that. The Sheriff's Department has been less than forthcoming with me," Learner told her.

"I'll check it out, Chief. I've gotta go follow up on that burglary case over by the Fire Station anyway," Della replied.

It was a damned cold morning for Florida. He had dressed in long pants, a t-shirt from the Smoking Tuna Saloon and a light jacket. He checked his phone. The temperature in Miami was a brisk 40 degrees. They were talking on the news something about a polar vortex that was blasting its way south. The Midwest had temps close to the surface of Mars.

Having experienced below zero wind chills in New York, Marlow was hoping he wouldn't see them in Florida. He took the list he had printed out the night before from his pocket and studied it in the line at McDonalds.

The Escobars owned a lot of properties. Marlow checked the lists against a map of Miami as he waited. People moved forward. Marlow stepped forward too. He ordered coffee and sausage biscuits and gravy as well as a hash brown. Marlow carried them to a table and sat down. He opened the biscuits and poured the gravy over them. He added sweetener to the coffee and stirred it in along with a couple of cubes of ice.

Marlow wished that Dave Parker would call, but he wasn't counting on it. Parker was still pissed at him for breaking into the Escobar offices last night.

Marlow ate his breakfast as he studied the map. He tried to figure out where the girl was being held. She was out there somewhere.

Chapter Eleven

Stock Island, Florida Keys

Della Martin had driven across the bridge to where Phil Gordon had lived. What was left of his shack was a few smoking boards. A curtain moved in the trailer next door but no one ventured outside. She didn't see Gordon's truck anywhere but that didn't really mean he was gone. The curtain in the trailer moved again and Della felt a chill race down her spine. She backed out of the drive and headed back across the bridge to Key West.

Erik Vanderbilt's boat had been scuttled in the Bight the night before. By itself it didn't seem like much, but added to the torching and murder of Frankie, it was more than a coincidence. Especially given the fact that Erik was a SEAL back in Vietnam. He knew explosives. Explosives had been used on Phil Gordon's house. Payback? Likely.

The Coconut Telegraph had been very active about Phil Gordon after he had been arrested. Della needed to find out how all of that had started. It might point her toward the bombers and also towards Gordon himself!

Yet a part of her wasn't sure she wanted to deal with Gordon face to face. There was something about him that made her nervous. That he appeared to be a psychopath was only part of it. There was something almost reptilian about him that frightened her on an almost primeval level.

Della shook her head as she headed her car towards the Bight.

Phil Gordon watched the Lady Detective drive away. He wondered why she was on Stock Island. There was no way that anybody could connect him to what he had done the night before. He had been pretty careful, and he knew that there was no way she had seen his face when he had tried going after her.

He sipped at the beer that Donny had given him. He would lay low until dark, then it would be time for another trip across the bridge to the island. More payback was owed him.

"Della? This is Dr. Harmon. I got your message, what can I do for you?" Dr. Jessica Harmon's voice spoke into her ear.

"I need to see you. Somebody tried to attack me last night, I pretty much lost it afterward," Della admitted.

"I can see how that would bother you. Did you get drunk?"

"I did. It seemed the easiest thing to do."

"What if your attacker had followed you?"

"He probably would have gotten me," Della sighed.

"Crawling into a bottle is not the answer," Dr. Harmon told her.

"I know that," Della sighed.

"Yet you did it anyway."

"I did. It somehow seemed safer than facing it," Della shrugged.

"But it wasn't really, was it?"

"No, it wasn't. I need to be better Doc."

"I know that. You do too. I have an opening at 3 p.m. I'll be looking for you then."

"I'll be there," Della told her and then broke the connection. She swung into Harpoon Harry's and ordered a *café con leche*. She drank the sugary coffee drink.

Miami, Florida

Rick Marlow sipped at his coffee as he sat outside one of the addresses that he had gotten from the offices of the Escobar Brothers the night before. A car pulled up to the curb behind him and Dave Parker emerged from the car. He walked over to the passenger side and climbed in.

"Slow day?" Marlow asked.

"Not so you'd notice," Parker replied. "You got anything yet?"

"Nothing worth mentioning," Marlow sighed.

"I figured as much," Parker noted.

"You don't have faith in me?" Marlow looked at him.

"No, I know the Escobars fairly well though," Parker replied, sipping at the cup of coffee he had brought with him.

"You do. And still you haven't managed to nail them for anything," Marlow noted.

"Believe me it is not for lack of trying," Parker sighed.

"I never thought it was," Marlow told him.

"I have people watching all their places. If they see the girl they will move," Parker told him.

"Good to know. Except I don't expect them to show her yet. They want to hook her on their product first, make her want it so bad she'll do anything for them to get it," Marlow told him.

"I don't disagree," Parker told him.

"I know," Marlow told him.

"So what are you going to do?"

"Keep watching," Marlow replied.

Andrea Gables groaned in pain. The man in the suit had beat her, hurt her. He had brutalized her in ways she had never imagined possible. But it was what he had whispered as he had done it that frightened her. Andy shivered in fear as the sun came up

Gomez Escobar frightened her. He had come in after the other one and things had gotten even worse. The threats he had whispered in her ear as he had forced himself on her. Tears filled her eyes. She knew that she would do what he asked of her, because to fail him meant that her mother would die.

She hurt from his treatment of her. Blood still leaked from her ass from where he had sodomized her. Her face hurt from where he had slapped her after she had pleasured him with her mouth. But he gave her drugs, drugs that erased the pain that she felt.

Andy whimpered into the sheets that had been left for her comfort.

She was pretty sure at this point that her chances for survival were limited. Nobody could prove different.

Marlow finished his coffee and climbed out of the car. He felt a need to stretch his legs. Dave Parker had left a long time before. He had driven back to the Escobar offices after Parker left. He didn't necessarily agree with Parker's assessment of the situation but he also knew it wasn't far off.

The 9mm was in his jacket pocket as he walked towards the building. Different guards this time and Marlow walked right to the desk.

"May I help you?" the man asked.

"I'd like to see Mr. Escobar," Marlow replied.

"Your name sir?"

"Marlow."

"One moment," the guard told him, reaching for a phone. He dialed an extension and then waited a few seconds. "I have a Mr. Marlow to see Mr. Escobar." He listened for a few seconds. "Certainly, I'll send him up," the guard said. Marlow smiled at him and strolled towards the elevators.

"Fifth floor," the guard called after him. Marlow merely nodded, already knowing which floor the offices were on. After all, he had visited them the night before. He entered the elevator and pressed 5 and then turned and watched as the doors closed.

When they opened he walked out into familiar surroundings. Marlow pretended to take a moment to orient himself. Then he walked towards the reception desk. A dark-haired Latino beauty sat behind the desk. She looked at him with undisguised curiosity. "I'm Marlow, to see Mr. Escobar," he told her.

"Which one?" she smiled. It was an enticing white smile showing perfect teeth. Amusement was evident in her eyes.

"Whichever one is in," Marlow shrugged, showing her a crooked grin of his own.

"What if they both are?" she teased him.

"In that case I'd like to see them both."

"Regarding?"

"That is for their ears alone," Marlow said mysteriously.

"Really?" she raised an eyebrow.

"Really," Marlow nodded.

"Mr. Marlow is here," she winked at him as she stabbed a button on a box on her desk. An accented voice replied.

"Send him in," it said.

Simon Escobar stood to greet him, dressed in a black suit with a white shirt and skinny black tie. His salt and pepper hair was slicked back against his skull and a thick dark mustache covered his lip. A cigar smoldered in the ashtray on his desk. "Mr. Marlow, what may I do for you?" Escobar asked.

"Do you employ a man on Key West named Phil Gordon?" Marlow asked.

"We employ many people," Escobar waved his hand dismissively.

"Well old Phil called your personal attorney to get him out of jail. You seem to be his only client. Other than Phil Gordon and old Phil has no means to hire such a lawyer," Marlow shrugged.

"Perhaps they are friends?" Escobar shrugged.

"No, according to the Key West Police Department, Frances Bertram represents Phil Gordon because you pay him to do so. You see Phil is in a lot of trouble for kidnapping and having sex with underage girls. One of them vanished right before he was arrested, and then suddenly your lawyer shows up to get him out of jail," Marlow said. "It makes me wonder."

"Wonder about what? A silly coincidence?" Escobar blew out smoke.

"Is it?" Marlow looked at him.

"What else?"

"A conspiracy maybe? Possible Mann Act violations?"

"Are you a policeman, Mr. Marlow?"

"I'm a private investigator," Marlow confessed.

"Then I really don't need to speak to you at all."

"Not even out of curiosity?"

"Get out of here before I have security remove you," Escobar asked.

"I won't go away Simon. Think about that. Until I have that girl back safe and sound, I will haunt you," Marlow told him.

"You might just end up dead," Escobar hissed.

"Was that a threat, Simon?" Marlow asked, raising an eyebrow.

"A prophecy."

"Have a nice day," Marlow told him and turned and walked out. The door had no sooner closed behind him than Simon Escobar was dialing his brother's number on his cell phone.

Marlow smiled at the secretary/receptionist on his way out and she smiled back. Promising, he decided. He walked to the elevator and rode it back down to the lobby.

He had rattled Simon, and badly. The question now was what would Simon do? Marlow climbed into his car and drove to a nearby McDonalds for lunch and to go to the bathroom.

"Phil Gordon is a problem that needs to be eliminated. Take care of it," Simon Escobar ordered.

"I told you this might happen," Frances Bertram shook his head.

"You did. Until now, Gordon was a useful tool. Now he is not. I want him dead by sundown," Simon Escobar ordered.

"I'll set it in motion," Bertram said. He broke the connection. Bertram snarled a curse and reached for his rolodex. There were people he could call to take care of Gordon. However it would have been better if the Escobars had listened to him when he first had become concerned about Phil Gordon.

Chapter Twelve

Gomez Escobar parked his Mercedes in the parking lot across from his offices. He whistled a happy tune as he climbed out of the car and ambled across the street. Gomez was shorter than his brother and younger, not showing any gray yet in his hair or the neatly trimmed goatee he sported. This morning he was wearing a pastel blue silk suit over a pale blue shirt with a tie the same color as his jacket. Dark-lensed sunglasses covered his eyes.

He jangled the change in his pocket as he walked. The sun was hot as he crossed the street. And he could feel sweat beading on his forehead before he stepped through the door into the cool air-conditioning where the sweat quickly evaporated. Gomez waved to the guard and entered the elevator, stabbing the button for the fifth floor with his forefinger. The doors hissed closed and he felt the tug of gravity as the elevator started to rise.

Selena was behind her desk as Gomez stepped off the elevator. She looked down at her desk as he walked passed her and entered his brother's office unannounced. Simon looked up at him his eyes blazing with fury. "Where the hell have you been?" Simon demanded.

"Relaxing," Gomez waved his hand languidly to dismiss the question.

"That idiot Gordon and the new girl have brought trouble down on us!" Simon hissed angrily.

"How?" Gomez looked amused. He was remembering his time with the girl.

"Gordon was arrested for kidnapping and child molestation yesterday. His house was blown up by angry peons! Our offices were burglarized last night, and a private investigator came here to question me today!" Simon spat.

"So kill them," Gomez yawned.

"Bertram will take care of Gordon. We need to take care of this Marlow guy!"

"What do you want me to do, Simon?" Gomez looked at his older brother.

Marlow had watched Gomez Escobar walk into the building and snapped a few pictures with his digital camera. He would e-mail them to Walter and have them sent back to his motel. Gomez interested him. He had a strong gut feeling that Gomez was the one that had taken such a strong personal interest in Andy Gables.

Marlow shook out a cigarette and lit it. He thought it was number 3 for the day. He started his car and headed back for the motel. He needed some sleep. He would come back closer to closing time. He had the impression that he might be able to get something from the secretary receptionist if he played his cards right.

Erik Vanderbilt looked across the table at Dana. "Son of a bitch sunk my boat last night, Dana. How the fuck did he know?"

"I don't know Erik. I'm sorry. What can I do to help?" Dana asked.

"Can you bring Frankie back to life?" Erik glared at her.

"No, nobody can do that," Dana looked down at the tabletop.

"This asshole is coming after us all. How can we stop him?" Erik asked.

"Only way I can think of is to kill him," Dana shrugged.

"That might not be a bad idea," Erik said coldly.

"Erik, think about this for a minute," Dana started to put her hand on him then stopped when he glared at her. She had forgotten that Erik and Frankie had dated for awhile. She thought about it. She would, she decided feel the same way if anything had been done to Corrine.

"I've given it all the thought I need to. Cops said Frankie was beat to death before the bastard burned him. He's gonna pay for that. I don't give a shit about the boat, but Gordon's gotta pay for what he did to Frankie," Erik said.

"Phil Gordon has to pay for a lot of people," Dana said, thinking of her friends that Gordon had raped and beaten.

"Have everybody start looking for him. First one that spots him calls me," Erik looked at her.

"I'll spread the word," Dana nodded. Erik nodded his head, took a long pull on his beer and kept looking off into space. Dana slid from her seat and walked off. She needed to stop by and see Corrine first, and then she would start spreading the word...

Della looked at Dr. Harmon. Today, Dr. Harmon was wearing a soft mint green tropical sundress that brought out both her flawless tan and blue eyes. She was wear clog sandals and looked totally relaxed. A white shell necklace hung around her neck. She brushed back her reddish brown hair until it caught behind her ear. She had an amused expression as she looked over the frames of her glasses.

"I've been feeling really shaky the past week or so. Last night I was off work when the fire trucks went past. I walked down Duval and one of the t-shirt shops across from Mallory Square was burning. My boss said the owner was probably inside.

"I wasn't on call so I didn't catch the case. I knew the two detectives that did, so I headed back to my car. I had a funny feeling that I was being watched, but didn't notice anyone paying any particular attention to me. My car was parked four blocks away. I was getting close when I heard footsteps behind me. I looked back and didn't see anyone. So I kept walking, but the footsteps were getting closer. My heart started racing and my hands were shaking as I walked. Finally I drew my gun and turned.

"I saw a man step into the shadows and disappear. I stood there, my gun pointing at the shadows where he had vanished. I couldn't see his face, but his shape seemed familiar. I got in my car and locked it, then drove home as fast as I could and got into my house and made sure every door and window was locked and the security system was armed.

"I was sweating and it was a cold sweat. I sat down and waited for my hands to stop shaking, then I turned on the stereo and poured myself a drink. I started drinking and I woke up on the couch this morning," Della explained.

"How did you feel this morning?" Harmon asked her voice low and pleasant.

"Awful. The hangover wasn't the worst part of it. The worst part of it was the depth of the fear and the fact that when I woke up, it was still with me," Della said, her own voice pitched low.

"How did that make you feel?"

"Sick. It was like right after the shooting all over again, jumping at shadows," Della shook her head.

"You don't like being afraid. You think it makes you less than what you think you are," Dr. Harmon observed.

"Something like that," Della sighed.

"It's tough being a cop isn't it. A woman in what has always traditionally been a man's role. Even with the stride made in gender equality, you still feel like you have to work harder, try harder, be better than the male officers in order to get and keep their respect. You feel like showing any sign of weakness will cause you to lose that respect. Your relationship with Marlow is making your boss doubt your proven abilities and the stress is getting worse instead of better. Add to that the fact that you were being stalked last night, and your reaction is perfectly understandable and under the circumstances quite normal," Dr. Harmon explained.

"You have a way of making it sound simple. Yes, I am scared and yes, I am stressed. I'm wondering if I went back to work too soon after the shooting," Della sighed. She felt almost like crying.

"Nothing is ever as simple as it sounds. I would think that would have been one of the first things they would have taught you at the Police Academy," Dr. Harmon told her.

"Why was I so afraid last night?" Della asked, meeting her therapists' eyes.

"You were thrust from a relaxed mindset into a danger mindset in a matter of moments. Your cop instincts were in overdrive after hearing a murder had been committed. Walking back in the dark took you emotionally back to the parking lot of The Chart Room on the night you got shot in the parking lot. When the stalker appeared and you recognized the danger, something you had missed the night you were shot. After you faced it, and the adrenaline rush ended, you had an emotional breakdown. Just a small one, but enough to make you drink more than you normally would," Dr. Harmon explained.

"Will it happen again?" Della asked.

"That is up to you. But if it does, we'll work on it together. Time's up Della. Same time next week?" Dr. Harmon looked at her.

"Yes," Della nodded as she stood and walked out.

Corrine Taylor smiled and waved at Dana when she walked into The Smoking Tuna Saloon. Corrine hadn't been working there long but the customers were cool, the tips were good and her hours were flexible. Plus her boss didn't mind when Dana came in to see her. Corrine had short blond hair and a ready smile with a slight overbite. She had a slightly upturned nose and a smattering of freckles over a cupid's bow mouth.

"Hi Corry," Dana smiled ad gave her a quick kiss on the cheek.

"You want a beer?" Corrine asked with a grin.

"Not now. I have some stuff I have to do," Dana shook her head.

Like what?" Corrine asked.

"There are some people I need to talk to about some stuff that happened on the beach the other day," Dana shrugged.

"It have to do with the fire over at Frankie's last night?"

"I don't know. It might," Dana sighed.

"You know something? 'Cause the cops are saying Frankie was murdered before the place was burned."

"I heard that too. Hey, if Phil Gordon comes in, call me. And stay away from him. He's dangerous," Dana told her.

"Why do you want to know if that asshole comes in?" Corrine had seen Phil Gordon in action and had fended off a few of his advances before he figured out she preferred girls to boys.

"Just call me," Dana pleaded.

"Okay," Corrine promised.

"I love you Baby," Dana told her before turning and heading for the door. Corrine watched her go, suddenly afraid for her girlfriend.

Stock Island.

"You have anything wit' that mess over on Key West last night?" Donny asked Phil Gordon.

"You're asking a lot of questions all of the sudden," Phil glared at him as he downed a Pabst Blue Ribbon from the can.

"Figure it's yo' business, but it could come back on me if anybody figures out where yo' stayin'," Donny shrugged. He took a swig of his own PBR.

"Fuckers blew up my house. You suddenly think they ain't got it coming?" Gordon looked at him through hooded eyes.

"No, I figure they got it comin' all right. You going over there again tonight?"

"I still got unfinished business on Key West," Gordon said.

"They's a bike chained up in the shed outback. You use it, they ain't gonna notice you like if you take your truck again. That Truck stands out," Donny told him.

"You gotta key to the padlock?" Gordon asked.

"I wouldn't a brought it up if I didn't," Donny cackled.

Phil Gordon shook his head. The old man was starting to get on his nerves. Plus, Phil wasn't so sure the old man wouldn't sell him out when he headed for Miami. He'd have to think on that some more. Gordon crushed the empty can and walked to the fridge and got out another one.

Miami, Florida

Marlow sipped from the Styrofoam cup of coffee he had bought at a nearby 7-Eleven. He had also eaten a couple of Ham and Cheese sandwiches and a bag of Lays potato chips. It was nearly five o'clock and time for the offices of the Escobar brothers to close. Many people were filing out but there was only one that Marlow was interested in. The secretary/receptionist. Marlow didn't know her name but he knew what she looked like.

He figured she knew a lot more than she let on. People in her position were often ignored and heard and knew a lot more than their bosses thought. He figured if he could get her to talk away from the office, she might be a bit more forthcoming than when he had met her in the office. He watched her as she exited the building and crossed to the parking lot. She climbed into a metallic blue Mini-Cooper with a white roof and white stripes on the hood. He started his own car and when she pulled out onto the street, Marlow pulled out behind her.

Chapter Thirteen

Marlow left his rental parked at the curb as he walked up the sidewalk. He had purchased a bottle of Champagne earlier and he carried it in his left hand. He knocked on the door of the apartment he had seen the lady from Escobar's office enter. A moment later the door opened and he was once again looking into those big brown eyes.

"Yes?" she asked him, her voice having much less of the accent she had spoken with at the office.

"Remember me?" Marlow held up the bottle of bubbly.

"You are the man that made Simon so angry. That was very foolish of you, Mr. ..." she let it hang.

"Marlow, Rick Marlow. This is for you," Marlow handed her the bottle. She examined the label.

"You have taste, Mr. Marlow. I'm Carmen Dezugnia. Come inside please and we can share this," Carmen smiled at him. She opened the door wider and Marlow stepped inside.

"Thank you for inviting me Carmen. You said making Simon Escobar angry was dangerous. What did you mean by that?" Marlow asked as he followed her into a spacious living room. Tasteful Spanish-themed artwork hung on white walls. Flowered patterned curtains covered the windows. The coffee table was glass and the furniture was white and soft. A large screen television and DVD player were hooked up to a satellite box. A tall bookcase stood along one wall and Marlow could see it was stocked with more than just romance novels. There were books on law as well as some mystery novels by well-known Florida authors. Carmen handed him back the bottle and asked him to open while she went to get them proper glasses to drink from.

Marlow stripped off the foil and slowly twisted out the cork. It came out with a soft pop. Carmen walked back into the room carrying two Champaign flutes.

"Congratulations on not spilling it on my carpet. Otherwise I'd had to bill you for the cleaning. The landlord isn't very understanding," Carmen smiled at him as Marlow filled first her glass and then his own.

"So why is making Simon angry dangerous?" Marlow asked again as he took a chair and she sat down on the white couch across from him.

"Simon and his brother are very dangerous men, Mr. Marlow. Such men it is not wise to trifle with," Carmen closed her eyes and took a sip of her drink.

"You sound almost like that comes from experience," Marlow observed.

"Why were you at the office today, Mr. Marlow? What did you say that made Simon so angry?" Carmen asked.

"I'm a private investigator," Marlow said.

"You smelled like a cop," Carmen nodded to herself.

"You know something about Simon and Gomez Escobar," Marlow looked at her, taking a sip of his drink. The bottle sat on the table between them.

"Both of them are pigs, hijo de putas! Some days it is like fending off a pair of octopi!" Carmen sighed.

"Did you know they are trafficking in women?" Marlow asked.

"It would not surprise me," Carmen took another sip.

"I'm looking for a girl that they might have taken. Have you ever heard of a man named Phil Gordon?" Marlow asked.

"Yes. He is a pervert. When he comes around he rapes me with his eyes. I don't like him," Carmen shivered. Marlow didn't tell her that he agreed with her character assessment of Phil Gordon.

"What else are they in to?" Marlow asked.

"I don't know for sure, but I suspect they are trafficking drugs as well as young girls," Carmon looked at her polished toes. She had slipped off her shoes as they talked.

"Any idea where they might be sending the girls?" Marlow took another sip of his drink.

"South Beach. Gomez frequently writes checks to a Sandoval Enterprises in South Beach," Carmen sighed. Her shoulders dropped as if a burden had been lifted.

"You have a personal reason for hating them don't you?" Marlow asked suddenly.

"Si, I do. My sister met Gomez in a club. She vanished shortly afterwards. I never heard from her again," Carmen replied.

"If I can find her, Carmen, I will," Marlow told her.

"I think perhaps, if anyone can, Senor Marlow, it will be you."

"Here is my cell number. If you find anything, call me," Marlow slipped his business card across the table to her.

"Thank you for the Champagne Marlow. Perhaps we will meet again," Carmen smiled at him. Marlow smiled back and stood, and then let himself out the door. He had learned a lot, more than he had expected.

Margaret Harrison sipped her cosmopolitan. Brad had done a good job of mixing the drink. She frowned, despite the elegance of the evening. The new girl had arrived and she had been badly used. If it was by Simon or Gomez or both, she didn't know, but she was pretty sure it was one or the other. If not both. Dr. Morgan had given her a sedative and done what she could.

Margaret took another drink. Simon and Gomez were beginning to become a problem, even if they did supply her with girls. She needed to do something about that. Perhaps it was time to let her bosses know that the Escobar brothers were becoming a problem.

Key West, Florida

Thom Hark leaned back in his chair. He had been following the rumors about Phil Gordon that were up and down the Keys. He had also managed to connect the explosion of Gordon's house to the rumors. There had also been the fire at Frankie's t-shirt shop and the murder there.

Rumor had it that Marlow was interested in Phil Gordon. Thom wanted to know why. He picked up his phone and he dialed Walter Loomis.

The sun was starting to go down and Della Martin was sitting in her car. She was looking for Erik Vanderbilt. Erik was an older guy, but he and Frankie had once been lovers. Della had a feeling that Erik knew something about Gordon's house blowing up. So she was looking for Erik.

Della knew a few places where Erik liked to hang out. The Schooner was one of them. She put her car in gear and drove over there and parked out front. The fact that she was a cop allowed her to double park without a problem.

Della locked the doors on her car as she shouldered her purse and headed inside. Erik Vanderbilt sat on a stool in the Schooner. His mug was full as he sat there. He spotted Della but didn't bother to acknowledge her.

"Hey Della," Erik said.

"Nice to see you Erik. How have you been?" Della asked.

"Not so great. You hear about Frankie?"

"I did. I know you two had been close," Della acknowledged.

"We split but I still cared about him. Why would somebody do that to him?" Erik took another slug of his beer.

"Anger? Revenge? Maybe because their house was blown up?" Della asked lightly. Erik looked at her, his eyes like marbles in his face.

"My boat got sunk last night. Anybody looking into that?" Erik almost growled at her.

"Erik, don't do something stupid. Getting yourself killed or arrested won't bring Frankie back."

"You think I don't know that?" Erik looked at her, tears in his eyes.

"You know anything about what happened over on Stock Island yesterday?"

"Talk to Dana Vincent. She's the one told us about Gordon," Erik sighed.

"Us?" Della looked at him.

"I've told you all I'm going to. Maybe it's time I left here. Key West is getting too damned dangerous for my taste," Erik drained his beer and sat the empty on the bar. Then he slid off the stool and walked away, leaving Della sitting there.

Corrine Taylor walked over to where Della was sitting. "Erik is taking Frankie's death pretty hard," she said.

"I can see that. You know where Dana is tonight? Erik suggested that I talk to her," Della said lightly.

"About what?" Corrine asked.

"That house exploding over on Stock Island yesterday. Said she knew something about Phil Gordon," Della shrugged. She knew Corrine and Dana were a couple.

"Shit. I was afraid Dana was caught up in that. She hates Phil Gordon and after word got out he was raping young girls and beating them, she made sure everybody knew about it. Phil Gordon isn't welcome anywhere on Key West," Corrine shook her head. "It's funny, she was in here earlier and asked me to keep an eye out for Gordon. Almost like she was expecting him to come around."

"Corrine, Dana may be in a lot of danger. I think Phil Gordon is out to get everyone involved in blowing up his house. I think Dana and Erik were part of that. Where is Dana?" Della demanded.

"Let me call her," Corrine pulled out her cell phone.

"Do that," Della told her.

112

Phil Gordon had peddled across the bridge at sunset. He left the bike in a stand and stayed off Duval unless he could easily blend with the crowds. He was wearing dark slacks and a black t-shirt tonight. Tonight he was looking for both the lady cop and Erik Vanderbilt. He had sunk the guy's boat last night, but he hadn't been on it. He aimed to correct that mistake tonight.

The crowds were thick and swirling in and out of each bar and club along Duval. Gordon stayed with them. He had no idea he was being hunted as well. He spotted Erik Vanderbilt as the man staggered out of the Schooner into the street, heading towards the Bight.

Gordon followed discreetly. Finally they were away from the crowds and there were plenty of shadows to hide in if he needed them. Gordon didn't think he did. Erik Vanderbilt was obviously drunk off his ass and could barely walk a straight fucking line.

Gordon smiled. This was gonna be easier than he had thought! They were almost to the Bight when he drew the .357 revolver out from under his shirt. He had gotten it from Donny, making sure that the old man knew that if Gordon went down he would take the old black man with him.

Gordon aimed at the old man staggering along ahead of him, just the two of them in the dark. Erik Vanderbilt stopped and turned around to face him. "I ain't that easy, Gordon. You're gonna have to look me in the fucking eyes when you kill me," Erik told him.

"I got no problem with that," Gordon said as his finger tightened on the revolver's trigger.

Suddenly gunfire was filling the night and bullets were cracking the air around him as Vanderbilt drew and fired a very loud big-bore gun. Gordon fired back, as he dived for cover. Bullets sent splinters into his face as he rolled behind a wooden piling. Gordon fired around the piling. He heard a grunt and Vanderbilt tumbled to the ground. Gordon fired again, hearing the bullets thud into yielding flesh. He threw the gun into the water and ran back towards Duval Street.

Erik Vanderbilt lay on the ground. He had dropped the Colt Government Model .45 that he had carried since Vietnam. He could feel the life oozing out of him. He touched his fingers in the bloody pool leaking out of him and wrote Phil Gordon's name. Blood bubbled from his lips as he tried to laugh after naming his killer.

Dana Vincent was in the Green Parrot when her phone rang. She had come here because it was one of Phil Gordon's favorite hangouts. She had hoped to see him and call Erik to let him know where Gordon was, however Gordon had never shown. She was disappointed.

Her cell phone rang. Dana pulled it out of her pocket and looked at the number. It was Corry. Maybe news about Gordon. She answered it. "Hey Corry," she said.

"Della Martin is here. She wants to talk to you," Corry told her.

"Put her on," Dana sighed.

"Dana, talk to me about Stock Island," Della said.

"Fuck," Dana groaned.

"Erik told me to talk to you. What do you know?" Della demanded.

"I'm at the Green Parrot. Come here and I'll talk," Dana whispered. She broke the connection. She was in trouble and she knew it. She hoped it wouldn't spill over onto Corrine.

Chapter Fourteen

"What may I do for you Thom?" Walter Loomis asked when he answered the telephone.

"Where's Marlow?" Thom asked his tone urgent.

"Miami, I believe. Why?" Walter asked.

"He asked me to do some checking on both the Escobar Brothers and Harold Gables. What I found was not good! The brothers are very dangerous criminals, though so far they haven't been caught. A contact at the Miami Herald did some deep background on them. Harold Gables is on his second marriage. The first one ended after he was accused of molesting his daughter by his first wife. Harold barely escaped jail in that one," Hark informed him.

"Marlow suspected as much about Gables. It would certainly explain his attitude towards Andrea Gables. Can you e-mail Marlow what you have and I'll give him a call to alert him that it is on the way," Walter replied.

"I can do that," Thom nodded, even though he knew Walter couldn't see him. He broke the connection and turned back to his computer.

"It's bad Chief," Detective Leo Margolis told him as Tom Learner stepped out of his car. Margolis was average height with dark curly hair that lay close to his head. He had brown eyes and a thick mustache that covered his upper lip. He was wearing a blue Aloha shirt outside his khaki slacks. A pair of white walking shoes covered his feet. Margolis was actually off duty but had heard the shots and responded.

"You identify him yet?" Learner asked as he walked towards the body.

"Looks like Erik Vanderbilt but I haven't checked the body for I.D. yet," Margolis replied.

"Shit. Call Della, get her over here now. She was gonna talk to him earlier about his boat sinking," Learner ordered.

"Sure thing, Chief," Margolis pulled out his cell phone and dialed Della's number. Learner knelt down on the pavement next to the body, being careful to stay out of the blood pooling around it. It was Erik Vanderbilt all right. Learner noticed the Colt Government Model .45 nearby. It looked like the gun he knew Vanderbilt carried and had a permit for. Maybe the dead man had gotten lucky and tagged his killer. It would sure make him easier to find. He grabbed his radio-mike and called for the Crime Scene Unit.

A couple of minutes later Margolis was back. "Della's on the way Chief. Should be here in a couple of minutes."

"Thanks Leo. Good to know. Don't let anybody get near the body until the CSU's get here," Learner told him. Learner needed a moment to think. He pulled a cigar from his pocket and bit the end off of it. He lit it a moment later with a Zippo that his father had given him the day he joined the Marines. It bore the crest of the Corps engraved into the metal.

This was no co-incidence. Frankie Tomlinson last night, Erik Vanderbilt tonight. Tomlinson's shop being burnt down, Vanderbilt's boat being scuttled in the Bight. Tom Learner knew he wasn't the sharpest pencil in the box, but that was why he hired people who were smart. There was also the matter of Phil Gordon's house being blown up the day before. This seemed a lot like a revenge killing, 'cept ol' Erik had put up more of a fight than Frankie had.

Tom Learner blew out a cloud of smoke. One thing was for sure, Marlow wasn't involved this time. He guessed he owed that old boy an apology this time. Della would like that. She had feelings for Marlow and they had been keeping company over the past few months. Maybe he was jealous. Della was a beautiful woman, and a damn good cop. Every man on the force had tried getting in her pants, and she never gave a single one a tumble. Then Marlow came along.

The former New York cop had managed to do what none of the local boys could. He caught Della's attention. It was ego more than anything else that had made him dislike Marlow. Plus the boy was smart, and often made Tom feel like some redneck dipstick. That wasn't Marlow's fault though. It was his. Learner took another puff on his cigar. About that time, Della pulled up, the MARS light on the roof of her car flashing. Learner turned to meet her.

Della was halfway to the Green Parrot when her cell phone rang. She looked at the readout on the display. Leo Margolis? She hit answer. "Yes, Leo?"

"Sorry to bother you Della, but Chief wants you over hear by the Bight. Erik Vanderbilt's been shot," Leo told her.

"He still alive?"

"No, one of the reasons the Chief wants you. Said you were talking to him earlier," Leo told her.

"Tell the Chief I'm on my way," Della broke the connection. Dana Vincent would have to wait, at least for a little while. Della ran back to her car and climbed in and started it up and headed towards the Bight.

She saw the lights from the Chief's car first and followed them to the scene. She pulled in beside him. Tom was leaning on his front fender smoking a cigar. Della shut off her engine and climbed out of the car. She walked around to where he waited.

"Chief, you called?" Della asked, knowing it was a stupid question even as she asked it.

"I did. Erik Vanderbilt was shot multiple times. You talk to him earlier?" Learner asked.

"Yes. He gave me a name and I was on my way to question that person when Leo called," Della replied.

"That name can wait a bit. Erik tell you anything else?"

"He figured Phil Gordon for sinking his boat."

"You think he might be right?"

"I do. Erik admitted to helping blow up Gordon's house said the name he gave me was behind it," Della replied.

"He say why they did it?"

"Because Gordon was a Chicken Hawk, preying on underage girls," Della sighed.

"How did that get out?"

"I don't know," Della admitted.

"Might be a good thing to find out. Put out a Be On the Look Out for Phillip Gordon. I want his ass in a holding cell before morning," Tom Learner told her.

"I'll get that B.O.L.O. out Chief. Looks like the CSU boys are getting here," Della told him. A van bearing the initials C.S.U. pulled into the lot and the Medical Examiner's hearse was right behind them.

"Get on it then, I've got a crime scene to supervise," Learner said. Della nodded and headed back to her car. She needed to catch up to Dana Vincent at the Green Parrot and see what she had to say. On the way she used the radio in her car to call in the B.O.L.O. on Phil Gordon. With luck he would be in custody before morning!

Phil Gordon stayed to the shadows. That damned Fag had nearly got him. He had been forced to go into a bathroom and pull some wood splinters out of his face. A few blood dots showed where he had removed them. God that had been a rush, shooting the old man that way!

Gordon took a deep breath and let it out slowly. This was the biggest high he had ever found. He needed release and soon. Gordon headed for the Green Parrot. He needed a drink to take the edge off and calm him down.

Miami, Florida

Margaret looked down at Andrea Gables. She was sleeping peacefully. Margaret sipped at her glass of wine. She felt sorry for the girl, she truly did. Margaret had been through it herself. She remembered her father starting his nightly visits to her room. She remembered drawing away from her friends. Even Rick, her best friend. She knew his dad was a cop and could help her, but she couldn't tell him what was happening. She was too ashamed. Then one day her father had taken her for a drive and handed her off to a man named Fred.

Fred had been a pig, he had raped her repeatedly before passing her along to a man named Squires. Squires had cleaned her up, got her counseling and sent her to school. He had brought her along and trained her to be a first class whore and then a first class Madam.

She still worked for Squires. She ran his Miami houses for him. He had contracted the Escobars to supply girls for him. Most of them were okay, they knew what they were getting into. Some of them had no idea. Those were highly addicted to heroin or cocaine. She had turned most of them back out onto the street pretty quick. Word had it that they had vanished and the Escobars had made it happen.

Andrea Gables reminded her of herself at that age. She wasn't going to turn her out onto the streets. Margaret had already called a specialist in addiction and she was working to slowly wean Andrea off of whatever kind of shit that the Escobars had injected into her veins. No, this girl was going to get a chance at survival!

Rick Marlow sat at the bar. He had fired up his fourth cigarette of the day as he enjoyed a Killian's Red. The first one of the night. Carmen Dezugnia had given him more than he had hoped. He now knew beyond any shadow of a doubt that the Escobars were behind the kidnapping of Andrea Gables.

The big question was why? What possible motive could they have for arranging for the kidnapping of Andrea Gables? He was pretty sure the answer would lie with Harold Gables. Gables was guilty of something, more than maybe molesting his own daughter.

Marlow blew out smoke rings as he considered that. He pulled out his cell phone and dialed Dave Parker.

"Parker," the detective answered.

"Who are the top Madame's in Miami?" Marlow asked.

"You that desperate to get laid?" Parker cracked.

"Not so much. However it might well explain why the Escobars are having girls shipped in from Key West."

"Importing talent?"

"Could be. It would certainly explain a lot," Marlow replied.

"You seem pretty sure of that."

"I am," Marlow replied.

"I guess it could bear worth looking into," Parker nodded.

"It does," Marlow told him.

Key West, Florida

Phil Gordon bellied up to the bar in the Green Parrot. He looked around but nobody seemed to take any notice of him. That was a good thing. He ordered a beer and drained half of it in a single gulp. He turned and looked around the bar. Dana Vincent was over in a corner looking miserable. Fucking Dyke. He owed her one, but this wasn't the place to deal with her. He saw her head start to turn and looked away from her so that she didn't recognize him.

He had an idea that maybe she might be part of his problem. He remembered the beat down she had given him a year ago. All over some split tail that he had had some fun with. Gordon drained the beer and ordered another. He kept watch on Dana out of the corner of his eye.

She kept looking at her watch like she was waiting on somebody. That was interesting. He took another pull on his beer, but he was being careful now. He wanted to see who Dana Vincent was waiting on. Maybe somebody involved with blowing up his house and his current troubles on the island.

It was a good thought. He was hungry for a woman. Maybe Dana, maybe the lady cop, maybe somebody random. It didn't matter. He would find some relief tonight. He missed Andrea, but she had got him into this damn mess.

Della Martin pulled up in front of the Green Parrot. She was surprised that the Chief had let her leave a scene he so obviously needed her on, but then again, he had assigned her to this one. She parked her car in a side lot and locked it before heading inside the Green Parrot.

She knew Dana Vincent, knew she was a friend of Marlow's. Corrine had pointed her towards Dana for a reason. Della knew that the two women were lovers and were involved even now. The loud music slapped her like a fist when she stepped through the doors, making her pause and cringe for a moment.

Her brown eyes surveyed the room. She spotted Dana in a corner and made her way over to her. "Dana, we need to talk," Della told her.

"Yeah, I know we do," Dana sighed, gulping down the rest of her drink.

"You want to talk here or down at the station?" Della asked.

"We'll start here I guess. Phil Gordon killed Frankie and Erik," Dana told her.

"Why?" Della asked.

"Because we blew up his house."

Chapter Fifteen

"**W**ow," Della said. Dana looked miserable as she stirred the straw around in her drink. "Marlow told me about him kidnapping that little girl, raping her and addicting her to drugs. Phil Gordon had raped a friend of mine last year. When she told me I kicked the shit out of him. Gordon stayed away from me and her after that," Dana told her.

"Why did you blow up his house?" Della asked softly, her eyes watching the room behind them.

"We wanted to send him a message. We wanted him to know that he was no longer welcome in Key West," Dana told her.

"Did Marlow put you up to that?" Della asked.

"Marlow knew nothing about it," Dana shook her head. "I went to Erik and Frankie. Frankie ran him out of his place right after he got released from jail."

"Frankie was the first to die. Gordon's revenge for what he saw as disrespect. Good God, Dana! You set off a chain of murder and violence. What the hell were you thinking," Della shook her head.

"I thought we might get rid of that son of a bitch for good," Dana whispered. Della looked at her and shook her head.

"Dana, I have no choice but to arrest you. You understand that don't you?" Della sighed.

"I know. What we did was wrong, even though we did it for the right reasons," Dana nodded.

"Okay then, I am not going to cuff you. I'm going to trust you to go with me willingly," Della told her.

"No problem," Dana stood. Della stood as well and they headed towards the door, unaware they were both being watched and followed.

Phil Gordon had nursed his beer as he watched the Lady Cop talk to Dana Vincent. He had no idea what they were saying but he knew neither of them was happy. He could tell that much from their faces. Finally they stood and headed for the door. Gordon tossed a twenty on the bar and headed outside after them.

Miami, Florida

Dave Parker hung up the phone. He had spoken to Marty Fly over in Vice and had gotten a list of names for Marlow. He recognized a lot of them. He would never have connected any of them to the Escobar brothers. The missing girl was the priority. As he looked at the list, he tried to figure out which of the Madame's would be the most likely to be harboring the girl sent to her by the Escobars. He picked three off the list.

Parker picked up his cell phone and dialed Marlow's number. Once the Key West Private Eye answered, Parker read him the list of names. He also told Marlow the ones he figured were most likely. Then he broke the connection.

Rick Marlow looked at the list in his hand. One name stood out. Margaret Lawson. He wondered. Could it be? His head swam as he thought about it. He put his rental car in drive and headed for the address he had written down beneath the name.

Margaret Lawson sat her drink down. The bell summoned her to the foyer. Only Malachi would give that particular signal. Simon Escobar was waiting on her as she entered the room.

"How is she?" he asked.

"Not good," Margaret replied disdainfully. She had no love or even like for the Cuban.

"She will improve?" Simon asked.

"Eventually," Margaret replied.

"And what do you think?" Simon looked into her eyes.

"I think you and your brother abused her badly. It will take time for her to recover," Margaret sniffed as she took a sip of her drink.

"You think we were wrong to do so?" Simon looked at her.

"What I think doesn't matter, obviously," Margaret looked away, not meeting his gaze.

"So true. I want her ready to move in three days," Simon said.

"Then you shouldn't have used her like you did! She has issues now, Simon," Margaret told him.

"Her issues are nothing. She will do what I ask or she will die," Simon shrugged.

"You care that little?" Margaret asked.

"I don't care at all. Gomez is the one with feelings for her," Simon shrugged.

"And why is that?" Margaret exhaled smoke in twin streams from her delicate nostrils.

"He looks to her as **a** means to an end," Simon shrugged.

"What end?" Margaret sipped at her drink.

"He covets her mother who is married to one of our employees. I think it amuses him that he can take them away from this man who tries to hold that he is superior to us who hold the power. Gomez wishes to rub his nose in how easily he can take what the man has," Simon tasted his own drink.

"Interesting," Margaret murmured.

"Three days. Not a moment longer or you don't get paid," Simon drained his drink, stood and walked out leaving her sitting there. He didn't see the predatory smile she flashed in his wake.

Marlow pulled up across the street from the rather magnificent old house that fit the address he had gotten from Dave Parker. The moon was full and bloated in the night sky. Marlow turned off the headlights and shut off the motor of his rental. He wanted to observe for a bit before approaching the house. A car pulled out from a long drive. It looked familiar. It drove past him and Marlow recognized Simon Escobar.

Interesting. What would Simon Escobar be doing at a whorehouse? Obviously the man didn't need to pay for sex. He was also married. The two didn't mean he wasn't a patron. Perhaps he had some personal kinks he didn't want his wife to know about?

It was something to consider. Marlow fired up a cigarette and sat there in the dark smoking it. Traffic moved at a fairly regular pace in and out of the drive. If Parker knew about this place other cops did too. Why hadn't Vice raided it and closed it down? Obvious answer, it had protection, which meant somebody high up was getting paid to look the other way.

He thought about calling Parker again but decided against it. He was pretty sure he knew why the detective had given him this address. Marlow was no longer a cop and he could do things that Parker could not, go places in pursuit of the Escobars that Parker could not. "Well played, Parker," Marlow said as he ground out his cigarette in the rental car's ashtray.

Marlow climbed out of the car and locked it, then started across the street. The night was warm and muggy, holding the promise of rain though so far there were no visible clouds in the sky. He walked across the wide lawn to the front door and rang the bell.

Key West, Florida

Phil Gordon followed the two women out into the dark parking lot. He stayed in the shadows as they moved towards the Lady cop's car. He smiled as he quietly moved up behind them. He drew his gun from under his shirt and held it ready in his hand as he closed the difference between them. The Lady Cop was in the rear. Gordon slammed his gun into the Lady Cop's head and she dropped like a rock. He grabbed Dana and slammed her into a car, digging the muzzle of his gun up under her jaw on the left side.

"Hello, Bitch! I heard you were one of the ones that blew my fucking house up!" Gordon snarled, spittle flying from his lips into her face.

"Fuck you, Phil! You deserve every bad thing that happens to you," Dana spat in his face.

"Bitch!" Gordon slapped her across the face with his pistol, drawing blood from a long cut on her cheek.

"What's the matter, Gordon? You can't take insults from a girl?" Dana snarled at him.

"Listen you fucking dyke, I'm gonna show you what a man can do," Gordon said as he unzipped his pants. He slapped her hard with the pistol again, stunning her. Phil Gordon lowered her to the ground and tore down her shorts and underpants. He thought about shoving the gun up her snatch and pulling the trigger, but didn't. No this fucking Dyke was gonna have a real man. He spread her legs and thrust himself into her, feeling her squirm and scream as his manhood tore into her.

Gordon grabbed her by the throat and squeezed hard as he rammed himself into her. He kept squeezing and thrusting until he exploded inside her. He pulled out and she lay there, her head cocked at an odd angle.

"You motherfucker!" Della's voice snarled from turned to look behind him. Phil Gordon saw the muzzle of her gun pointed at his head.

"She asked for it," Phil said.

"Fuck you, asshole!" Della pulled the trigger and Phil Gordon's head exploded into crimson mist! Della rocked back on her heels, panting for breath. Gordon's blood covered her face. Della looked at Dana Vincent and knew immediately she was dead. Gordon had broken her neck as he had raped her. Della put her gun on the ground and dug in her purse for her cell phone. She dialed the Chief.

"Learner," he said crisply as he answered the phone.

"Phil Gordon is dead. Caught him raping and murdering Dana Vincent," Della whispered.

"Where are you, Della?" Learner asked.

"Parking lot outside the Green Parrot," Della said before she broke the connection. She dropped her phone back in her purse.

Tom Learner climbed out of the car, his red and blue mars lights flashing, painting the scene in a hellish hue. Della was leaning against a car, a couple of uniformed officers on each side. Blood was splattered across her face and her blouse and jacket. Bits of gray brain matter as well. What remained of Phil Gordon had collapsed on the body of Dana Vincent who's head canted to the left at an unnatural angle. Her eyes were wide open and starring up at the night sky. Her face was also covered with blood and brains.

"Della," Tom said to her.

"Chief?" she looked up at him questioningly.

"You okay?" he asked softly.

"No," Della shook her head. Learner looked at one of the uniforms.

"Call Jessica Harmon, tell her it's about Della and a shooting and I need her here right away," Learner said. The officer scrambled to make the call. Learner shrugged out of his jacket and put it around her shoulders. He could hear the ambulance in the distance. "You want me to call Marlow?"

"Call Walter Loomis. I need him," Della sighed.

"Hello?" Walter Loomis answered the phone, rubbing the sleep from his eyes.

"Walter? Tom Learner. Della Martin is asking for you," Learner told him.

"Why?" Walter still fighting sleep was puzzled.

"Della just shot and killed Phil Gordon while he was raping and murdering a witness," Tom said.

"My God! How is she?" Walter asked.

"Not well. Can you get a hold of Marlow? I hate to say it, but I think she needs him," Tom Learner sighed.

"I'll give Ricky a Call and then I will get there as soon as I humanly can," Walter Loomis replied. He broke the connection and dialed Marlow's number.

Tom Learner sat down next to Della. "I'm sorry," he told her.

"You didn't do anything, Tom," Della shook her head.

"I never should have given you this case," Learner told her.

"I think I'm going to throw up now," Della said and then she did.

Chapter Sixteen

Miami, Florida

A well-dressed butler let Marlow inside and guided him to a chair in an elegant foyer. He promised to let the Mistress of the house know that she had a visitor. Marlow waited about five minutes before she entered the foyer. She was tall anyway, but four-inch heels added to her formidable height. An emerald green gown hugged her curves in all the right places. Long red hair hung down and around her shoulders. "Ricky?" she gasped as she saw his face.

"Maggie?" Marlow whispered.

"My God," she whispered.

"Good to know you aren't dead," Marlow told her.

"For me as well," she told him.

"I suppose so. Dad arrested your father after you disappeared," Marlow said.

"Good to know. That fucking bastard deserved it for what he did to me," Maggie nodded.

"Yeah, I get that," Marlow nodded.

"I'm sure you do," Maggie agreed.

"You here to sample the wares?" Maggie raised a red eyebrow.

"I'm here to find a young girl sold into the life by Simon Escobar," Marlow shrugged.

"You know Simon?" Maggie looked at him, her green eyes searching his blue ones.

"Yeah, I think he and his brother took the girl I am looking for, a runaway from Key West," Marlow told her.

"That certainly sounds like them, Maggie nodded, sipping her drink.

"You know for a fact that they have done this before?"

"I do."

"What are you going to do about it?" Marlow looked at her.

"Come back tomorrow night Rick. I'll have something for you then," Maggie almost whispered.

"I'll be here," Marlow stood.

"It's been nice seeing you again, Ricky," Maggie stood as well, smiling. She stepped forward and gave him a hug. Marlow returned it.

Then he turned and left the room, heading on out the door to his rental car.

Maggie Lawson finished her drink. That had been an interesting and welcome encounter. She and Marlow had been friends as kids. As close as a brother and sister until her father had started molesting her at the tender age of twelve. She had just started budding into womanhood. She had been frightened that first night that he had come to her room in the night. She had tried to fight until he threatened to kill both her and her mother. Then she had let him have his way.

It had hurt. God how it had hurt. But the pain eventually went away. She had withdrawn from her friends, ashamed of what she was doing, having no idea at the time that it was not her fault. That her father was just a sick bastard who couldn't help himself. Then he had sent her away. She heard a few years later that he had been arrested and then murdered while in prison. Maggie didn't shed any tears when she got the news.

She climbed the stairs to the second floor to check on the girl named Andrea Gables. Dr. Townsend was still in the room watching over her and looked up as Maggie entered.

"She's resting. She will hurt for the next few days. The animals that used her, well children will not be something she will ever have to worry about," Gloria Townsend shook her head.

"I'm sorry to hear that. How soon can she travel?" Maggie asked.

"Maybe tomorrow, the next day at the latest."

"Good, then she has a chance. A friend of mine is coming to get her. He'll keep her safe," Maggie told her.

"Somebody needs too," Townsend said softly.

"The friend I am having take her out of here will make the ones who did this to her pay," Maggie said.

"I hope so," Gloria Townsend replied.

Key West, Florida

The ambulances had arrived and Tom Learner still wasn't sure what to do. The Crime Scene Unit from the Sheriff's department had arrived and were photographing everything. Della was sitting on the back bumper of an ambulance with a blanket wrapped around her shoulders. She wasn't talking anymore and Tom figured that might be a good thing.

He wasn't sure that Della should be talking. Not until Walter Loomis arrived. So much death in such a short time. Marlow wasn't on the island so he couldn't even blame him for it. No, this time, if he had listened to Marlow it might all have been avoided. Headlights crossed the parking lot. Walter Loomis stepped out of the car. Tom Learner breathed a sigh of relief.

"Where's Della?" Walter asked immediately. Tom pointed towards the ambulances. An EMT was trying to talk to her but Della stared mutely into space. Walter hurried over to her and was immediately appalled by her physical condition. Blood and bone and brain matter still decorated her face. He gave the EMT a hard look and the man stepped back.

"Della. It's me, Walter. I'd like to wash your face off if I may," Walter said in a soothing voice. She looked at him, her brown eyes wide and frightened. Walter took an alcohol-soaked wipe and washed the blood and other debris from her face.

"W-Walter?" Della gazed into his eyes and then threw her arms around his neck.

"Not a word, Della. Not until after the doctors have had a look at you," Walter told her.

"Rick?" she asked.

"On his way back from Miami as we speak," Walter assured her.

"Good. I need him," Della whispered.

"We all do," Walter patted her shoulder reassuringly.

Tom Learner sighed. The shit was going to hit big time in a big way on this one. Another car arrived and Thom

Hark stepped out of it. The situation had just gone from catastrophic to worse! Della climbed on into the ambulance and the doors shut behind her. The siren began to wind up as it pulled away. Thom Hark went straight to Walter Loomis and Tom Learner let loose a loud groan.

"What happened here, Walter?" Thom Hark asked.

"Apparently Detective Martin came upon Phillip Gordon while he was raping and murdering Dana Vincent and shot him in the head, but unfortunately not before Gordon had snapped Ms. Vincent's neck," Walter said. "Detective retained my services since she did not trust the local Police Chief to provide her with a decent defense attorney," Walter replied.

"I can understand her belief there," Thom nodded shooting Learner a look. The bespectacled reporter had no love for the Chief of Police or any of his cronies at City Hall. "Do you think this has anything to do with the Escobar brothers?"

"According to Marlow, Gordon was working for them as a procurer," Walter replied.

"Would he be willing to say that out loud?" Hark asked suddenly alert.

"You'll have to ask him that yourself when he gets here. He's driving down from Miami as we speak," Walter looked slightly annoyed. "Let's not forget my primary concern is Della and not whatever Marlow might be able to tell you."

"I'm sorry Walter, in my enthusiasm for the story I forgot myself. How is Della?" Hark said softly.

"In shock by my estimation. Ahh, there is Dr. Harmon. I suspect she can get Della to agree to go to the hospital and get checked out. Excuse me, Thom," Walter said as he waddled off leaving the reporter behind.

Walter dismissed the reporter from his mind as he hurried over to intercept Dr. Harmon before she reached Della. He wanted a moment to speak to her because he knew the Chief had called her in. He wanted to make sure that she would have Della's best interest at heart and not necessarily Chief Learner's.

"Jessica!" Walter called.

"Walter what are you doing here?" Harmon turned to face him. Her large brown eyes regarded him coolly. They knew each other well, Walter having once been a patient.

"I'm Della's counsel. She called and requested me, not believing that the Police Department would have her best interest at heart," Walter explained.

"I can understand that," Harmon nodded.

"I need to ask, Jessica. Are you here for Della or for the Chief?"

"I'm here for Della. She's been having some issues the past couple of days," Harmon replied.

"No doubt. I've heard a few things myself. At any rate, she's in shock and should be in a hospital," Walter told her.

"I agree completely," Jessica nodded. Walter walked her the rest of the way over to Della.

"Della, there's someone here to see you," Walter said gently. Della looked around and when she saw Jessica Harmon tears filled her eyes.

"Dr. Harmon," Della whispered.

"Take a deep breath and let it out slow," Harmon said.

Della did. She wiped her eyes with her hands. "I need help," Della said.

"First things first then. You need to go to the hospital and get checked out. Walter and I will meet you there and then we will talk," Dr. Harmon told her.

"But—" Della started.

"No buts, Della. Let the doctor's check you out and then we will talk. Anything will be confidential between you, me and Walter. You're covered," Dr. Harmon assured her. Behind her Walter nodded affirmatively. Della nodded her acceptance. One of the EMT's helped her up into the ambulance and got her comfortable on the gurney before closing the doors and the Ambulance started to roll away.

"Ride with me, Walter?" Dr. Harmon asked.

"Certainly, Jessica," he replied, following her to her car.

Miami, Florida

Marlow had just reached his car when his cell phone began to ring. He pulled it out of his pocket and looked at the screen. It was Walter. He answered it. "Walter, what's going on?" Marlow asked.

"There has been an incident. Della blew Phil Gordon's head off as he was raping and murdering another young woman. She's asking for you," Walter told him.

"I'm on my way, Walter."

"What about your case?"

"It can keep. Della's more important," Marlow told him, breaking the connection. He thought about what Maggie had told him. He had twenty-four hours. Plenty of time to go down to Key West and back...

Chapter Seventeen

Key West, Florida

It was well after midnight when Rick Marlow walked into the hospital room. It was dark, the only light coming from the steadily beeping monitors attached to all the wires and tubes attached to Della Martin. Quietly Marlow moved over to the bed and leaned over and kissed her softly on the forehead and then turned to look for a chair.

That was when he noticed the other occupant of the room. Dr. Jessica Harmon was sitting in a corner across from the door, hidden in shadows. Her finely sculpted legs were encased in pale white nylons, a dark skirt hit just above the knees and her wine colored blouse was slightly wrinkled. Her long dark hair hung in loose layers around her face. Dark framed glasses made her brown eyes look bigger.

"How is she, Dr. Harmon?" Marlow asked.

'In pretty rough shape, mentally and emotionally," Jessica Harmon replied.

"Did they sedate her?" Marlow asked, concern evident in his blue eyes.

"They did. She blew a man's head off inches from her own face as he was raping and murdering another woman and telling her that she was next," Harmon replied clinically.

"Who was the other woman?" Marlow asked absently.

"Dana Vincent," Jessica said. Marlow's head snapped up.

"Dana?" he barely whispered.

"You knew her too," Dr. Harmon observed.

"I did. Dana was a friend, a confidant even. We were close," Marlow sighed.

"Any sexual involvement?" Harmon had slipped back into clinical mode.

"Dana was a lesbian. We were like brother and sister," Marlow shook his head.

"Why was Dana with her? Apparently Gordon attacked them at the same time, apparently striking Della on the head first and stunning her, then he overpowered Dana and proceeded to rape her while choking her. Della apparently came to and put a bullet through his brain, but by then Dana was dead," Jessica told him.

"Fuck me running. I told Dana about Gordon, that he was raping and kidnapping teenage girls. I set this whole goddamn mess in motion," Marlow slid down the wall and buried his face in his hands.

"Rick it is not your fault. You were working a case and you needed someone to talk to. Della wasn't available and you spoke to Dana. You had no idea what she would do with what you told her if anything at all," Dr. Harmon said.

"And now four people are dead," Marlow rasped.

"Rick," Harmon said softly.

"Tell her I was here when she wakes up," Marlow said as he stood and walked out the door. Jessica fished her cell phone out of her purse and dialed Walter Loomis.

"Hello?" Walter Loomis sounded groggy and it took a moment for Jessica Harmon to realize she had awakened him from a deep sleep.

"Marlow was here. He's left already," Dr. Harmon said.

"How was he?" Walter asked.

"Concerned, upset. He said to tell Della he had been there and that he would be back."

"He came to make sure Della was all right for the moment, and now he has gone back to his dogged chase for the missing girl. There is something special about this case, Jessica. I don't know what it is though," Walter mused.

"Something from his past perhaps? Marlow is a man with a lot of pain and secrets. Many stemmed from his shooting, but there have been hints of older and deeper ones," Dr. Harmon suggested.

"And you think that might be behind his single-minded pursuit of this particular case?" Walter asked.

"I do. I suspect that this relates to something from Marlow's childhood. Something that none of us knows about," Dr. Harmon replied.

"How will we find out?" Walter asked.

"When Rick Marlow decides to tell us," Dr. Harmon sighed.

Rick Marlow entered his apartment. He flicked on the light switch and then locked the door behind him. He was tired, his eyes felt like they had sand in them. How many hours had he been awake? He couldn't remember. He stripped off his clothes and fell into bed. Tonight, he didn't even need a drink to fall into a deep sleep.

Sunlight was streaming intrusively through the window when Marlow opened his eyes, blinking rapidly to clear the sleep out of them. He sat up and rubbed the rest of it away. Naked he padded to the bathroom where he showered and shaved. Clean clothes followed and then he was out the door, driving over to Harpoon Harry's for breakfast.

As he ate and sipped at his coffee, Marlow thought about his day. He would go back by the hospital and check on Della before he headed back to Miami. Maggie would have an answer for him. He was pretty sure of that.

Seeing her had been a shock to say the least. Talking to her had brought back memories, ones that he really had no reason to want to revisit. Yet revisit them he had. In his own way, as a boy, he had been in love with Maggie. Not that he had realized it then, but afterwards, in retrospect he had understood.

Ron eyed him from a distance but had not approached, respecting the aura of privacy that Marlow had been exuding.

Normally the effervescent owner of the eatery greeted each patron personally, but today he had sensed Marlow's desire for privacy.

Marlow nodded to him as he paid for his meal and headed out the door. Della was his main concern at the moment. Marlow drove his rental across the bridge to Stock Island and the Medical Center there.

Miami, Florida

Andrea Gables opened her eyes. It was morning. But her memory was fuzzy. She sat up and was startled to realize that she wasn't alone. An older woman with flowing red hair sat in a nearby chair watching her.

"How are you feeling, Andrea?" the woman asked.

"Better. I still hurt, but I feel better," Andrea sighed.

"Glad to hear it. Do you want to stay with Simon and Gomez Escobar? Do you want to go through what you went through before again?"

"No, Ma'am. I just want to go someplace where they or my father can't touch me," Andrea shook her head.

"Your father?" Maggie asked.

"The bastard has been molesting me since I got breasts. I wish he was dead!" Andrea hissed.

"What if you could go somewhere else? Somewhere away from your parents as well?" Maggie looked at her.

"I would go in a heartbeat," Andrea said.

Key West, Florida

Marlow was sitting beside her when Della opened her eyes. "Good morning," Marlow smiled at her.

"Rick?" Della whispered, her voice raspy.

"I can't leave you alone for a minute, can I?" Marlow smiled again.

"I guess not. You hear about Dana?" Della asked, blinking back tears.

"Not your fault, Kid. It was mine. I never should have told her about Gordon," Marlow sighed.

"He broke her neck as I shot him. He was raping her as I shot him. He was the last thing she saw or felt. I let it happen, Rick!" Della sobbed.

"You couldn't have stopped him, Della. Gordon hit you on the head, knocked you out to take you out. He planned to do you next. But he recognized Dana, knew she had been the one behind blowing up his house," Marlow told her.

"Rick..." Della sobbed again.

"If anybody is to blame, Della, it's me. I was the one that told Dana about Gordon. Her death is on me," Marlow whispered. Then he stood. "I may have a lead on Andrea Gables. I have to go back to Miami. But I will be back," Marlow told her.

"Good luck," Della told him, meaning it. She watched Marlow leave. Despite what he had said, she took the blame for Dana Vincent's death.

She wished that she could dismiss the young woman's death as easily as Marlow. But she couldn't. Dana Vincent's death had touched her, hit her a sucker punch in the gut. Della wasn't so sure she would still be in Key West when Marlow got back.

Marlow fired up his first cigarette of the day as he drove away from the hospital. He realized that Della wanted to take the blame for Dana's death but she was not the one responsible. He was. It was he that had involved Dana. Marlow sighed as he exhaled twin streams of smoke. Coltrane's *Favorite Things* was playing on the radio as he headed back to Miami.

The sun was climbing rapidly as Marlow drove up Highway One. It was still early so there wasn't a lot of traffic. Another hour and that wouldn't be the case. Marlow's mood was dark. He was worried about Della, but Andrea Gables was foremost in his thoughts. And Maggie was there also. He sighed.

Miami, Florida

Maggie Lawson poured herself a cup of coffee. Aarons had put together an excellent breakfast. Maggie complimented him on it as he refilled her coffee. She had another twenty-four hours before Simon Escobar would come for the girl. Marlow would be back for her tonight.

Maggie thought about it for a while. Andrea Gables stood a far better chance with Marlow. He could keep her safe, from both her father and the Escobars. She picked up her phone and dialed Marlow's number.

"Hello?" Marlow answered the phone. He reached over and turned down the radio in the car. It was a lively Salsa number.

"Ricky? It's Maggie," Her voice was clear.

"Did you find her?" Marlow asked.

"I did," Maggie replied. "She wants to go with you. But she doesn't want to go back to her father. He's even worse than the Escobars," Maggie told him.

"I figured that much," Marlow replied.

"You were right. He's been raping her for years. The mother knew and did nothing," Maggie said.

"No, she was biding her time." Marlow said.

"So what are you going to do?" Maggie asked.

"Rescue the girl."

"How?"

"That, Maggie, is up to me," Marlow told her.

Chapter Eighteen

Rick Marlow pulled up once more in front of the building that houses the offices of the Escobar brothers. He wasn't sure yet what he was going to do. He fired up a cigarette and looked at the pack. One left. He put it back in his pocket.

Seeing Della like that, it brought back memories of when she had been shot. Except that damage had been more physical. This time it wasn't. This time it was mental and emotional. He knew she was already suffering from Post Traumatic Stress Syndrome from when she had been shot, and she had been making progress, but this? Marlow shook his head.

He knew he should call Dr. Harmon, get some advice for helping Della deal with everything. He had been glad to see her there with Della last night. He knew that his lover was in good hands. But Della's condition was one more mark against the Escobars.

Key West, Florida

Dr. Jessica Harmon sighed and took off her glasses, setting them on her desk. She found herself unable to concentrate and reached for the intercom. "Rosalie, cancel all my appointments for today, and then take the rest of the day off. I'm heading back to the hospital," she said.

"Yes, Doctor," her receptionist replied. Rosalie had been with her for several years and understood. Harmon was worried about Della Martin. They had spoken for a bit when Della had awakened and she had told Della that Marlow had come to check on her. But even that did little to cheer the detective up. Harmon had left orders for Della to be kept in the hospital under observation for the next couple of days.

She was deeply concerned for the young woman. Harmon slid her glasses back on her face and stood, smoothing her white skirt. Grabbing her purse and cell phone, Harmon headed for the door.

"How are you feeling, Della?" Thom Hark asked as he approached the hospital bed. Della didn't look good. Her eyes were red and swollen but she made the effort to smile for him. He carried the small vase of colorful flowers over and placed them on the stand next to the bed.

"Not my best day, Thom. Hope you didn't drag along a photographer," Della said softly.

"You look as beautiful as ever. Marlow called me and told me what happened. I wanted to make sure for myself that you were indeed okay," Thom sat down beside her.

"I don't know if I'm okay Thom," Della shook her head.

"Do you want to talk about it?"

"Not if it's going to end up on the front page of The Citizen," Della sighed.

"Strictly between us as friends," Hark assured her.

"You know about this case Marlow's been working?" Della looked at him.

"The Gables girl?" Thom raised an eyebrow quizzically.

"That's the one," Della nodded. "He had told Dana Vincent about Gordon and she put it out on the Coconut Telegraph. Apparently she and Frankie and Eric wired Gordon's house to explode after Frankie ran him out of his shop. Gordon missed getting blown up and came back to teach Frankie a lesson. He beat him to death and then burned down his shop.

"Phil Gordon also sank Eric's boat in the Bight. He came back the next night and killed Eric, then he saw me with Dana. He jumped us outside the Green Parrot and knocked me out. I came too as he was raping and choking Dana Vincent to death. I got my gun out and told him to stop. He told me to wait my turn and I shot him. Thom, God Help me, I wanted to kill him! And I did," Della's voice broke into a series of sobs. Thom Hark stood and slipped his arms around her, holding Della as she cried.

"You did what any cop would have done, Della," Thom told her after she finally stopped crying.

"A man wouldn't have been caught by surprise," Della shook her head.

"You can't know that," Thom said.

"I've always had to try harder than any of the men on the force. I failed, Thom," Della shook her head.

"Who are you?" a female voice asked from the doorway. Thom looked at the woman standing in the doorway. She was a striking brunette with brown eyes, a heart-shaped face, dark-rimmed glasses in an expensive white dress and jacket. White hose covered her shapely legs and white heels covered her feet.

"He's a friend, Jessica," Della cut in. Thom Hark stood and extended his hand.

"I don't believe I have had the pleasure," Thom smiled.

"Dr. Jessica Harmon. I'm her psychiatrist," Jessica replied.

"Thom Hark," he said by way of introduction.

"I know who you are, Mr. Hark. I don't believe Della should be talking to members of the press. I'm sure the Chief wouldn't want her to be giving any statements to the press in her condition," Harmon said coldly.

"Doctor Harmon, I am here as her friend. I'm also a friend to Marlow and to Walter Loomis. This once, I am not pursuing a story," Hark said haughtily.

"Be that as it may, Mr. Hark, your visit is at an end," Harmon said coldly.

"I don't want us to be adversaries, Dr. Harmon, so for now I will go. Della, if you need anything, anything at all, call me," Hark said looking at Della before walking out of the room.

"That was very rude of you, Jess," Della looked even more hurt.

"You need to be careful, Della. The Chief doesn't want you talking to the press right now," Dr. Harmon told her.

"The Chief can go fuck himself, Jess. I will talk to my friends any time I choose to."

"You need to be careful, Della. Right now your emotions are raw and bleeding. Anything that gets out will be used to try you in the court of public opinion," Harmon told her.

"What do you think, Jessica? You are my shrink after all," Della hissed.

"I think you are under a lot of stress, Della," Dr. Harmon said.

"You think?" Della rolled her eyes.

"I know."

"You think I can't trust my friends?"

"Are you sure you know who your friends are?"

"I am."

"I hope you're right," Dr. Harmon said.

"If you don't think so, then perhaps I need to find another doctor."

"Della."

"I mean it Jessica. If you don't believe me, I don't want you on my case," Della said.

Miami, Florida

Dave Parker rolled up beside Marlow's car. "Marlow, follow me," Parker called. Marlow nodded and started his car. He pulled out into traffic and followed the Miami-Dade detective. Parker drove a couple of blocks and pulled into a large parking lot. Marlow pulled in beside him and the two men exited their vehicles.

"What have you got?" Marlow asked.

"Escobar has put out a contract on you," Parker told him.

"Which one?"

"Both."

"So what's the going rate for murder in Miami?" Marlow asked.

"You've got a twenty-five thousand dollar price on your head," Parker told him.

"You figure somebody will try to cash in on it?" Marlow asked.

"Sooner or later," Parker acknowledged.

"So what do you want me to do?" Marlow took out the final cigarette and lit it.

"I suppose it would be too much to ask for you to get the hell out of Miami," Parker looked at him.

"Before I have Andrea Gables, yeah," Marlow blew smoke at Parker.

"I figured as fucking much," Parker shook his head in exasperation.

"Finding that girl is my job, Parker."

"Yeah, I get that."

"So, suggestions?"

"Aside from getting out of town?"

"Yeah?"

"Not really, no," Parker sighed.

"I thought as much," Marlow said.

"What the fuck are you going to do? I can't protect you, Marlow," Parker said.

"I'm not asking you to, Dave," Marlow replied.

"I know that Rick. But you're a friend and I don't want to lose you," Parker told him.

"I know," Marlow said.

Maggie Lawson stepped out of the shower. She hadn't slept much the night before. While she wanted to help both Marlow and the girl, the Escobars frightened her. They were brutal vicious animals with no redeeming qualities. Unfortunately, they were part of the cost of doing business in Miami.

She had been there a long time. Maybe too long. Perhaps it was time to move on? Would Marlow want her?

She might be able to trade on his past feelings for her for awhile. Maggie shook her head. No, that was something she couldn't do. She loved Marlow, loved the fact that he had cried when she had disappeared as a child.

No, if she left, it would be without his help. She would have to figure out how to do it on her own. Because she would have to elude her bosses as well...

Andrea Gables lay beside the pool, feeling the warm sun on her body. Her physical wounds had pretty much healed, but mentally and emotionally she was still a mess. She sat up and snatched a pack of cigarettes and a lighter. She shook out a smoke and stuck it in her mouth and fired the end of it.

Maggie had been nice to her. Gave her stuff to get her off what Phil had shot her up with. She still didn't understand why he had done that or why he had sent her to Gomez and Simon. They were both horrible and evil, the things they had done to her, Andrea let out another puff of smoke.

Maggie had told her about a man that would help her get away from Simon and Gomez. Who would help her get away from her parents as well, especially her father. The things he had done and forced her to do for him, they sickened her. Andrea put out the cigarette and made her decision. She would go talk to Maggie and tell her to call the man who could get her away.

Key West, Florida

157

"I'm worried about her, Walter," Tom Learner said. He was sitting in Walter Loomis' office, across the conference table from the elderly attorney.

"We all are Tom. Even Dr. Harmon is worried. Della has been wounded deeply by what happened to her the other night. It was a horrifying experience, compounded by what she went through earlier this year. I don't know many men who could have coped as well," Walter sighed.

"I can't let her come back to work until Dr. Harmon signs off that she's fit for duty."

"No, you can't. Hopefully Della will understand that and work with the Doctor."

"I don't know. Something is different about her now. I don't understand it or like it, but it's true. I heard Marlow came back down and saw her."

"He did Tom. However the case he's on forced him to go back to Miami," Walter replied.

"Don't ever tell him I said this, Walter, but I surely wish he had stayed. I have a bad feeling about Della."

Della Martin looked around her apartment. She had left the hospital on her own and caught a cab home. Except it didn't feel like home anymore. It felt foreign and cold. She wondered if she would ever be warm again.

Walking to the bathroom she stripped off the scrubs she had stolen at the hospital and turned on the shower. When the temperature felt right, she stepped inside and began to scrub at her skin as hard as she could. Maybe then the blood would go away...

Chapter Nineteen

Miami, Florida

Marlow took a drink from the bottle of water he had purchased from a convenience store. He had wished he had picked up another package of cigarettes, but he had made up his mind he was quitting for good. Part of the deal he had made with Della when they had finally started seeing each other. He smiled at the memory.

Della was a woman with firm convictions and beliefs. She didn't want to be second to booze or tobacco. Marlow couldn't say that he blamed her for that. He had been working on quitting smoking and had cut back a lot on his use of hard liquor. He hadn't given the vodka up entirely, but he had cut back. He was drinking more beer and wine these days, which Della certainly found more acceptable.

He didn't notice the white car rolling along the curb behind him until someone in the park screamed. Marlow dived for cover as gunfire erupted from the open windows. Wood splinters flew from the surface of the picnic table as Marlow clawed for the SCCY automatic holstered on his hip. Then the 9mm was in his hand and he was firing back at the car and it went screeching off.

Marlow climbed to his feet and looked around for his bottle of water. It lay spilling into the grass. He looked back in the direction that the car had disappeared. The shooters were long gone and he hadn't even gotten a real look at them. Marlow holstered his weapon and began checking one of the nearby bystanders to make sure no one had gotten hurt. He had a feeling that the Escobars had just upped the ante in their game.

Simon Escobar hung up the phone. He snarled a curse and yelled for his brother. Gomez sauntered in from the other office. He looked bored. "What?" Gomez asked.

"The men we hire failed to kill that insolent detective. I fear perhaps we might need to do this ourselves," Simon said.

"If we do, we do Brother," Gomez shrugged.

"Do you understand that his continued interference could cost us everything? Sometimes I think Mother should have drowned you at birth."

"You worry too much, Simon."

"You don't worry enough. You got us into all this, all because of that puta!"

"She is no whore! She is a good woman! Not that you would know," Gomez sniffed disparagingly.

"I don't care to. Though you certainly didn't object to sampling her daughter," Simon pointed out.

"Nor did you. And you were even rougher than I was."

"We need to find Marlow and kill him," Simon said.

Key West, Florida

Della Martin had dressed after her shower. Her hair was still wrapped in a towel. Art Pepper was playing on the CD player. She thought Winter Moon was the CD she had playing. Pepper was one of the greats. Della poured herself three fingers of whiskey. She added some ice cubes. It would water it down some. She took a sip, enjoying the burn from the liquor as it slid down to explode into her stomach.

She took another sip as the whiskey's warmth spread through her. How many people had died because of her? Not counting the ones she had actually shot on her own? Frankie. Kyle. Dana. And Phil Gordon. Four people dead in a couple of days all because of her.

Della stood and walked to her closet. Standing there for a long moment, she opened the door. On the shelf was a box. Della took the box and carried it to the living room and placed it on the coffee table. She took another drink and looked at the box. Slowly she reached down and opened it.

A Glock 19 sat in the box. Della took it out. She jettisoned the magazine. It was fully loaded. Della pulled the slide back and locked it open. She took another drink. She slipped the magazine back into the butt of the pistol until it locked in place. Della hit the slide release, chambering the top round off the magazine.

Della took another drink. She looked at the gun in her hand. Dana intruded into her thoughts. Screaming and crying, tears running down her cheeks as Phil Gordon raped her, thrusting himself deep inside her as his hand closed tighter around her throat. Della lifted the gun, placing the muzzle against her temple.

She took another drink, Dana's cries for help echoing in her ears. Tears streamed down Della's face. Her finger tightened on the trigger taking up the slack. Della took another drink. Dana's face haunted her as she fired the bullet that blew Phil Gordon's head off. Blood and brain and skull matter splattered against her face. Della squeezed the trigger one final time. Everything went black.

Miami, Florida

"Goddamn it Marlow! I told you this might happen!" Dave Parker roared in anger.

"Nobody was hurt," Marlow replied.

"Thank God for that," Parker sighed.

"I suppose," Marlow replied.

"I want you to get the fuck out of Miami, Marlow!" Parker told him.

"I'll be gone by tonight Dave," Marlow replied.

"You better be or I'll fucking arrest you myself," Parker glared at him. Marlow walked back to his car and drove to the same convenience store he had been at earlier. He bought another bottle of water and went back to his car. Where was he going to go now? He pulled out his phone and dialed Maggie Lawson. It was time to pick up Andrea Gables and take her home.

Maggie was waiting when Marlow arrived at the palatial mansion that housed her home and operation. She greeted her old friend with a hug.

"That was nice but what did it mean?" Marlow looked into her eyes.

"It means that I am sending Andrea with you. She trusts you because I do. Take care of her Marlow. She needs you, more than even she knows," Maggie told him.

"I know," Marlow told her, very aware of her closeness. Old feelings washed over him like a storm. Marlow looked into her eyes.

"No, Rick. That was a long time ago. Water under the bridge. As much as I wish we could, we can't go back there," Maggie whispered. Her eyes were filled with tears.

"Are you sure?" Marlow asked her.

"I am. You have someone in your life now. The detective you told me about."

"I do. But what we had..."

"Was a lifetime or two ago. Gone now, Rick, gone forever."

"Is it?"

"It is, Rick."

"Where is she?"

"Out by the pool. She's counting on you, Marlow. She wants a new life."

"Maggie, I'll do my best to help her. You know that."

"I do. She's had a hard life Marlow. She deserves better than what she's had."

"I know."

"Go take her. It won't be long before the Escobars come looking."

"I figured. Yeah, I guess it is time for us to go," Marlow nodded.

Key West, Florida

Jessica Harmon, dialed Della Martin's number one more time. Still no answer. She had been surprised to learn that Della had checked herself out of the hospital, though she wasn't sure why. Della was the type of person that would.

She hated being dependent on anyone. Jessica included. Jess shook her head frightened by what Della might have done. She climbed into her car and started the engine. She put the car in gear and headed for the apartment that Della kept on Columbia Street.

It was getting late. The sun was going down when Jessica Harmon pulled up in front of Della's home. She climbed out of her car. The wind was blowing from the south, carrying with it the scent of the sea.

Her relationship with Della and Marlow was a fragile one. It was not often that she counseled couples with a similar if not the same condition. And both were suffering from Post Traumatic Stress Syndrome. The fact that their relationship was the cause of it made it all the more interesting. Della still felt that Marlow was why she had been shot to begin with. Yet she loved the man, and it was pretty clear that Marlow felt the same about her.

Jessica shook her head. She wasn't sure of her own feelings about Marlow. He was a client after all. As was Della. Jessica walked to Della's door. She knocked, but there was no answer. Jessica waited. She wanted to help her friend.

Jessica Stood there confused. She could hear music playing through the door. Why wasn't Della answering? Was she in the shower? Jessica rang the bell again. Growing more concerned with every passing moment she pulled out her cell phone and dialed Chief Learner.

Miami, Florida

Marlow walked into the room where Andrea Gables waited. Andrea was dressed in a pair of red Capri pants and a green tank top. A pair of black ked-style sneakers covered her feet. She was chewing on a piece of gum and popping it occasionally. Her hair was clean and it had obviously seen the use of a curling iron. She looked at him appraisingly from half lowered lids that hid her green eyes.

"You the guy that's going to get me out of this mess?" she asked, popping her gum.

"I'm the guy that's going to try," Marlow nodded. "You ready to go?"

"Yeah, no point hanging around here anymore than I have to. Were those guys, the Escobars really going to turn me into a whore and a drug addict?"

"Probably."

"Did I make you uncomfortable talking that way?"

"Should it?"

"I don't know, that's why I asked. It always made Mama uncomfortable, especially when I told her how Papa used me. She would just shake her head and say that's a woman's lot in life. To be a whore for the man she married. I got the impression that she never really liked Papa all that much," Andrea replied watching his face.

"Did you get that impression before or after Harold started molesting you?" Marlow asked; his hands in his pockets.

Before, but it got worse after. That was when she really began to hate him. That was when she started calling me Daddy's little whore. Then Phil came along. He treated me good, better than at home. So I took off with him," Andrea shrugged.

"You couldn't catch a break could you? Because Phil used you and then sold you to the Escobars. Maggie told me what they did to you," Marlow told her softly.

"Yeah, he did. I hate that rat bastard!" Andrea's voice was filled with negative emotion.

"Would it make you feel better to know that Phil Gordon is dead?"

"It would," Andrea nodded, her curls bouncing.

"He is. He was killed last night by a policewoman that is a friend of mine down on Key West."

"Good. It serves the bastard right!" Andrea said vehemently.

"It's time to go," Marlow told her.

"Got a cigarette?" Andrea asked.

"Nope, I quit," Marlow replied. Together they left the house. Andrea eyed the rental car.

"That's your ride?" she looked over at him.

"It is," Marlow affirmed as he opened the door for her to climb inside. "Buckle up," he told her as he shut the door.

"I thought you private eyes always had fancy cars like Magnum or Rockford, or those guys on Hawaii Five-O," Andrea said as he climbed inside the car and started the engine.

"I used to have a Ford Pinto but it got blown up," Marlow   replied.

Key West, Florida

Tom Learner looked less than happy as he walked up on the porch to meet Dr. Harmon. "I guess she ain't answered the door yet?" Learner asked.

"You would be correct, Chief," Harmon answered. Learner nodded and pounded on the door. He gave it a few seconds and then pounded again.

"Della, it's Tom!" he yelled loudly. Still no answer. "Son of a bitch. Dr. Harmon you're my witness," Learner said as he reared back and kicked the door next to the locking mechanism. The door flew open. Tom drew his service pistol and led the way inside.

Chapter Twenty

Miami, Florida

Simon's eyes were smoldering with rage as they entered the house. Maggie was nowhere to be seen. Helena, her assistant approached the brothers. " How may we service you gentlemen tonight?" Helena smiled.

"The Gables girl. Where is she?" Simon demanded.

"I'm afraid she is gone. A man came and took her, said that she was wanted for a special order,' Helena said matter-of-factly. She was beginning to get a bad feeling. Maggie had also left without saying where she was going or when she would be back.

"Where is Margaret?" Simon demanded, shouting now. Bruno and Alexi stepped into the room. The two Russian's were the bouncers for the house.

"You need to leave, now!" Bruno said, his accent thick.

"I don't think so," Gomez said from behind Simon and then he shot and killed the Russian bouncer. Alexi froze.

"She left about an hour ago," Helena stammered.

"What about the girl?" Simon demanded.

"Gone about two hours ago. A man came and picked her up," Tears were streaming down Helena's face.

"Describe the man!" Simon ordered. She did.

"Marlow!" Simon hissed angrily.

"It is time for Marlow to die. He had interfered once too often," Gomez smiled. It was the smile of a shark, a predator that had scented blood in the water.

Simon shot the woman and killed her as Gomez shot the remaining bouncer. It looked like the whorehouse would be under new management. Simon and Gomez headed for their car. Gomez got on his cell phone and gave out Marlow's description. Their network would find him. However, Simon had a good idea where Marlow would go. Back to Key West. He headed for Highway One.

Key West, Florida

"Don't come in, Doctor," Tom Learner called over his shoulder. Art Pepper was still playing on the sound system. Learner didn't need the shrink to see what was left of Della Martin. The left side of her head was a gaping raw wound, her brains and skull and blood were splattered on the wall. A shadow filled the doorway. "God dammit Doc I said not to come in!" Learner yelled.

"You did. I don't know how I missed that she would do this," Harmon said distantly. Tears streamed down her cheeks as she looked at what was left of Della Martin.

"It's gonna have to be a closed casket service for sure," Learner shook his head.

"Is that all you can think about?" Jessica demanded, horrified at his callousness.

"Doc, just shut the fuck up," Learner sighed.

Somewhere on Highway One

"You don't talk about yourself much, do you?" Andrea asked.

"No, I don't," Marlow replied.

"Why is that?"

"I'm a private kind of guy."

"Sure you are," Andrea laughed.

"What do you want to know?" Marlow glanced over at her.

"What makes you tick, Marlow? You seem to be a nice guy, but I get the impression that if it comes down to it, you wouldn't be very nice at all," Andrea said.

"I used to be a cop up in New York, Andy. I got shot in the line of duty by my partner. I later found out why and took down the person responsible," Marlow shrugged.[2]

"Wow, I guess that makes you a regular hero," Andy smiled back at him.

"I'm no hero, Kid. I'm just a guy getting by," Marlow shook his head.

"Maggie says you'll help me," Andrea told him.

"I'm going to try," Marlow said.

"She likes you a lot," Andy told him.

"I know, Marlow replied.

"So why aren't you together?" Andy asked.

"Wrong place, wrong time," Marlow shrugged.

Key West, Florida

Tom Learner sighed. Dr. Harmon was starting to be a pain in the ass for him. Pretty soon Thom Hark and Walter Loomis would be inserting themselves into the investigation. Even though she had not left a note, Learner meant to leave no stone unturned.

---

[2] Marlow: The Neon Goodbye

For appearances sake, Tom let her stay. He did the same for a couple of local kids to whom Della was admittedly close.

Jessica Harmon sighed with relief. She had been sure that the chief would hurry her off. She dialed Walter Loomis. He had a right to know what was going on. So did Marlow. Marlow. Jessica shook her head. It would not go well once Marlow found out.

Along Highway One...

"Are we there yet?" Andy asked.

"Not yet," Marlow told her.

"How much longer?" she looked at him with a grin.

"Another hour," Marlow replied.

"So what's your big plan to save me?"

"I'm gonna play that by ear. I work for a lawyer that can certainly help."

"How?"

"I won't know until I talk to him," Marlow shrugged. His eyes were on the rearview mirror. Something in his face changed, alerting the girl that trouble was coming.

"What's wrong?"

"The Escobars are coming up fast behind us," Marlow replied calmly.

"Don't let them take me again!" Andy's voice was full of fear. Marlow spotted a turn off to one of the islands and powered through the turn leaving honking horns and squealing brakes behind him. He had to find a place that would allow him to hide the girl and take the fight to the Escobars. He hadn't caught the name of the island but it looked to be part of the park system. The paved road turned to gravel after a hundred yards and Marlow skidded onto it, throwing up a cloud of dust.

Cypress groves and weeping willows surrounded the car. Marlow spotted a turn and took it, the rental car bouncing over the rutted road. It ran out next to an old fishing shack built on stilts over the water. Marlow skidded the car to a stop. He shut off the engine and threw the door open. He glanced at the girl. "Out of the car, now!" Marlow ordered.

"Okay," Andy said, her face pale with fear. She scrambled out of the car. Marlow took her arm and half pushed her ahead of him towards the fishing shack.

Marlow ducked as the bullet hit the wooden wall and sent splinters flying in all directions. Behind him Andy whimpered and curled into a ball on the floor of the small fishing shack. Marlow waited until he could feel the tread of rubber-soled shoes on the wooden planking leading out from shore to where the shack stood on stilts that held it above the water.

The Escobars were coming. Marlow spun and leveled his revolver, the .38 bucking in his fist as he fired once, then a second time, before spinning back behind the wall. He heard a scream and then the sound of a body pitching into the water. There were curses in what he recognized as Spanish.

"Gringo! You are going to fucking die! Do you know this?" called a voice that he recognized as Simon. That meant he had shot Gomez.

"Fuck you Simon. Too bad about Gomez," Marlow called back. Automatic weapons fire ripped through the wooden walls. Marlow dived on top of the young red-haired woman that had gotten him into this mess, protecting her body with his.

Marlow had three shots left in his revolver, but he had the comforting weight of the SCCY automatic that Walter Loomis had given him on a previous case in his pocket. It held 11 rounds in it. He hoped that it would be enough.

Simon was on the walkway. Marlow lifted the .38 and fired the last 3 rounds. He heard Simon mutter a guttural curse. Splinters exploded from the doorframe and filled the air. Marlow shoved the .38 into his waistband as he dragged the 9mm auto out of his left hand pants pocket. Marlow switched hands.

The double action only 9mm was clenched in his right fist, chamber-loaded and ready to fire. Simon was coming. He could feel it.

The air was hot and thick with humidity. Sweat beaded on Marlow's forehead, dripping down into his eyes. He blinked it away. He could hear Andy Gables whimpering in fear somewhere behind him. The wooden bridge from land to the shack trembled slightly. Simon was edging closer. He could hear the Cuban hissing with rage as he edged closer. Marlow stood slowly, his fist tight around the grip of the little 9mm.

His heartbeat was loud in his ears. Simon Escobar would be expecting him to shoot from low. Marlow held the gun at chest level as he suddenly stepped into the doorway, catching Escobar by surprise and he squeezed through the trigger and the little pistol bucked in his fist. Simon stumbled backwards and Marlow fired again. The Cuban spun off the bridge and into the water, blood darkening the water around him. Marlow heard a snuffling grunt and then a salt-water crocodile had the Cuban's head in his mouth and did a death roll, taking the body below the surface.

Marlow turned toward where Gomez lay. He walked over and checked the body. His lucky shot had taken the man through the head. Gomez wouldn't be raping anymore little girls. Marlow headed back to the shack to get Andy Gables.

"Andy, it's over," Marlow said as he stepped back inside the fishing shack. He could see her sitting with her back against the wall, her knees drawn up and her arms wrapped around them. She raised her head and looked at him, tears streaming down her cheeks.

"Are they dead?" Andrea asked.

"They are," Marlow sighed.

"What are you going to do about Papa?"

"I'll think of something. Let's get out of here," Marlow extended his hand and helped her up. Together they walked back to the car. Marlow's phone started to ring.

Key West, Florida

Walter Loomis hung up the phone, his face pale. Lola Ponsberry carried him a cup of coffee. "What's wrong, Walter?" she asked, suddenly worried.

"That was Jessica Harmon. Della Martin committed suicide," Walter said.

"Oh my God!" Lola gasped, her hand going to her mouth.

"I need to call Ricky," Loomis said. He wasn't sure how Marlow would react to this news. He reached once more for the phone and dialed Marlow's number.

Marlow sat in the car unmoving. He broke the connection and slid his phone back into his shirt pocket. "What's the matter?" Andrea asked. Marlow didn't answer. He started the car and put it in gear and then turned it around and headed back for Highway One.

A storm was blowing in off the Gulf by the time Marlow reached Key West. He drove straight to the office. Lola hugged him when he walked inside leading the Gables girl. Marlow left the girl with Lola and walked to the conference room where he knew Walter would be waiting on him. Dr. Harmon was also there.

"I'm so sorry Rick," Dr. Harmon told him. Marlow ignored her and looked at Walter.

"We need to find a place for the girl and fix it so her parents can't have contact. Her father's been raping her since she was twelve. She cannot go back to that," Marlow's voice was a whispery rasp.

"I'll take care of it Ricky," Walter said gently.

"I know you will. Dr. Harmon, how could you let this happen?" Marlow's voice was fierce as he turned his anger towards the shrink. She flinched as if he had slapped her.

"I screwed up, Marlow. Simple as that. The signs were there but I missed them like some rank beginner just out of school."

"And Della paid the price. Somebody should have stopped her! Somebody should have been here for her!"

"Are we still talking about me, Marlow? Or are we talking about you?"

"I wish I knew," Marlow sighed.

Chapter Twenty-One

Rain beat down on the umbrella that Marlow held as he watched the coffin being lowered into the ground. He had stayed behind after everyone else had left. He grasped a handful of dirt and tossed it on top of the coffin. He pulled an unopened pack of cigarettes out of his shirt pocket. He tossed them into the grave and turned and walked to where Walter's car was parked, waiting for him. Marlow folded the umbrella before stepping into the car.

"Andrea Gables called and left a message. She likes the new boarding school. She said to tell you thank you," Walter told him. Marlow looked out the window.

"Glad to hear it," Marlow said. Walter started the car, turning on the windshield wipers. Art Pepper was playing Winter Moon on the radio as the car left the cemetery.

= = =

Coming Next

Last Mango In Paris

More children go missing in the United States every day. Some are kidnapped by non-custodial parents, some are killed by creeps that prey on them. Some fall victim to pedophiles. More than a few are sold into slavery and shipped around the country or overseas. Victims of Molestation almost never completely recover from what they have been put through. Sure, some do mange to go on to lead semi-healthy semi-normal lives. But the nightmares live on in their minds. South Florida has one of the largest transient populations in the United States, so a lot of kids fall through the cracks. It is a theme I have explored in other books I have written, and likely one I will look at again in the future because it is a national, even worldwide problem. Until something is being done to stop it, it will continue. Mango Run was a platform to call attention to it, as well as further highlighting the problem of post-traumatic stress and what it can do to a person. A reader told me that what happened within felt contrived and hurried. However, suicide is often a hasty decision made by those who can no longer face the demons in them and the feelings that had descended on them like an avalanche. It often does strike without warning and everyone close to the person is left wondering what he or she might have done to help or prevent it. Sadly there is often little that can be done by the time the person is ready to pull the trigger. That being said, I hope that you have enjoyed Marlow's latest case and will be looking forward to the next one.

Bill Craig
New Castle, IN
2014

Thank you for reading.
Please review this book. Reviews help others find me and inspires me to keep writing!

If you would like to be put on our email list to receive updates on new releases, contests, and promotions, please go to AbsolutelyAmazingEbooks.com and sign up.

About the Author

Bill Craig taught himself to read at age four and began writing his own stories at age six. He published his first novel at age 40 and says it only took him 34 years to become an overnight success! He has been publishing steadily ever since that first book *Valley of Death* and now has 27 books in print or ebook. Bill is the proud father of four children ranging in age from 38 to almost 8. He has 7 grandchildren and 1 great grandchild. Mr. Craig has worked a wide variety of jobs over the years from private security and corrections work to being a grill cook and dishwasher. He has been a news reporter, done factory work and even a stint as a railroad clerk. He currently does customer service work to support his writing addiction. His ultimate goal in life is to break the record held by pulp author and creator of *The Shadow*, Walter B. Gibson, for writing the most works in a single year!

ABSOLUTELY AMAZING eBOOKS

AbsolutelyAmazingEbooks.com
or AA-eBooks.com